Hello Nail,

As you will be traveling to Switzerland also in youre new job, I wanted to give you some reference material.

I also would like to thank you for our pleasant collaboration. It has been a pleasure to work with you, travel with you, meet your wonderful family and see your house. Take care and all the best.

Bye, Jeroen

ps. Would love to welcome you for dinner also in the future

Diccon Bewes and Michael Meister

How to be Swiss

Bergli

Diccon Bewes has lived in Switzerland for eleven years and is author of *Swiss Watching* and *Around Switzerland in 80 Maps*.

Michael Meister is a Swiss illustrator and cartoonist, who draws for companies and newspapers from Hong Kong to Zurich to New York.

MIX
Paper from
responsible sources
FSC® C068066

Printed in Switzerland by Schwabe AG, Muttenz
ISBN 978-3-03869-000-9
Also available as an e-book:
ISBN (epub) 978-3-03869-001-6
ISBN (mobi) 978-3-03869-002-3

Introduction

The art of being Swiss isn't an easy thing to master, even if you have a head start by being born that way, but this instruction manual will help you make it (or fake it). This eight-step programme is the result of years of hard work by the authors themselves, one British and one Swiss.

The first step to Helvetic heaven is often the toughest: how to greet the Swiss when you meet them. Once you've passed that test, the next takes you back in time through the history every Swiss knows (or should do). Further steps will have you living and laughing like the Swiss, seeing the world through their eyes, negotiating a political maze, and finding Swiss bliss in the simplest of things. Not forgetting the Swiss Commandments, which will be revealed in all their glory.

By the end you will have learnt how to enter a lift properly and discovered why 1908 was such a special year; you will know how to spend your Sundays and have navigated the Swiss archipelago. In fact, you will have realised how Swiss you are already, or how Swiss you want to be.

Step 1:
Meeting and greeting
Those moments when you negotiate the social minefield of making first contact, be that in a lift or on a train.

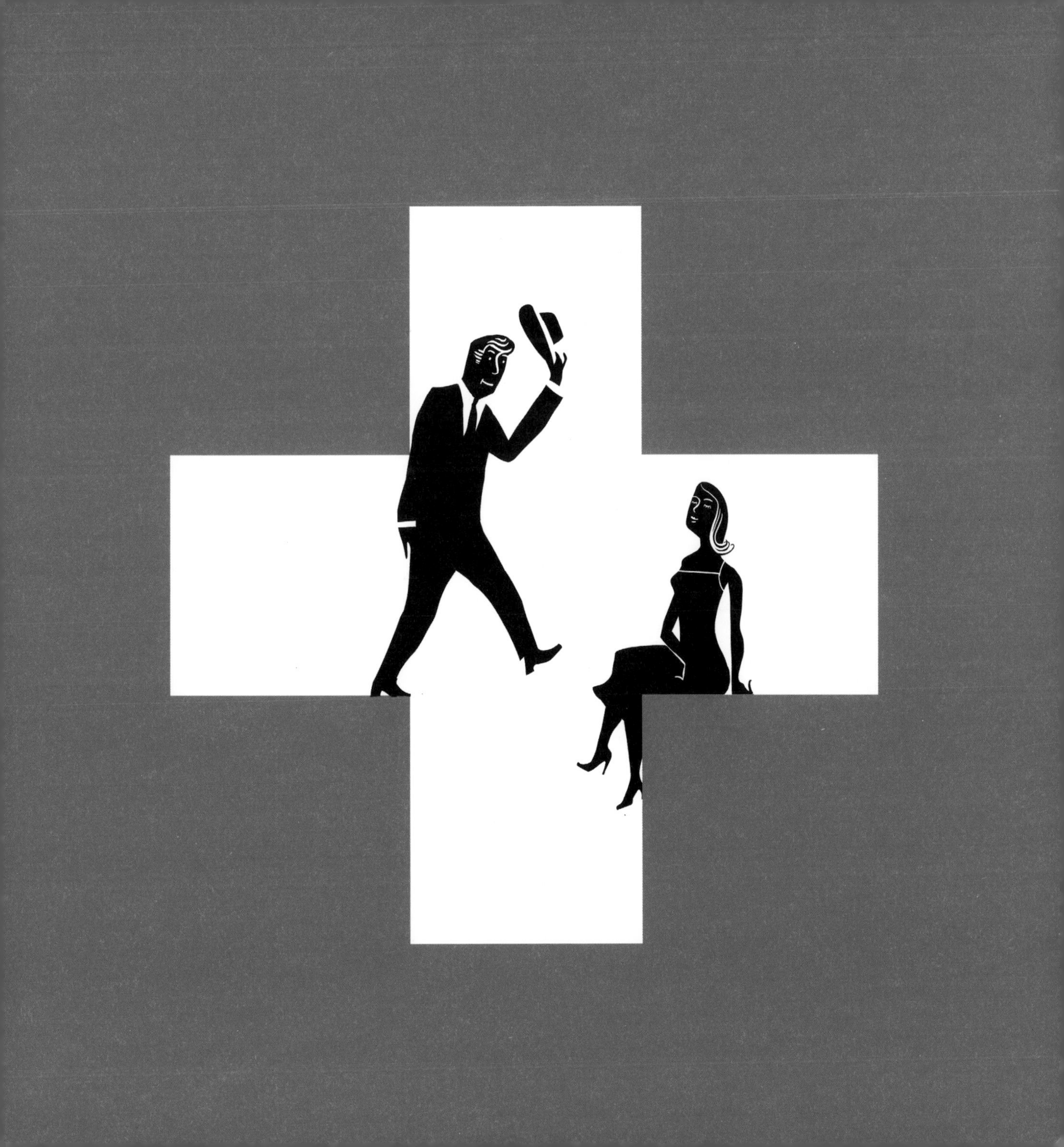

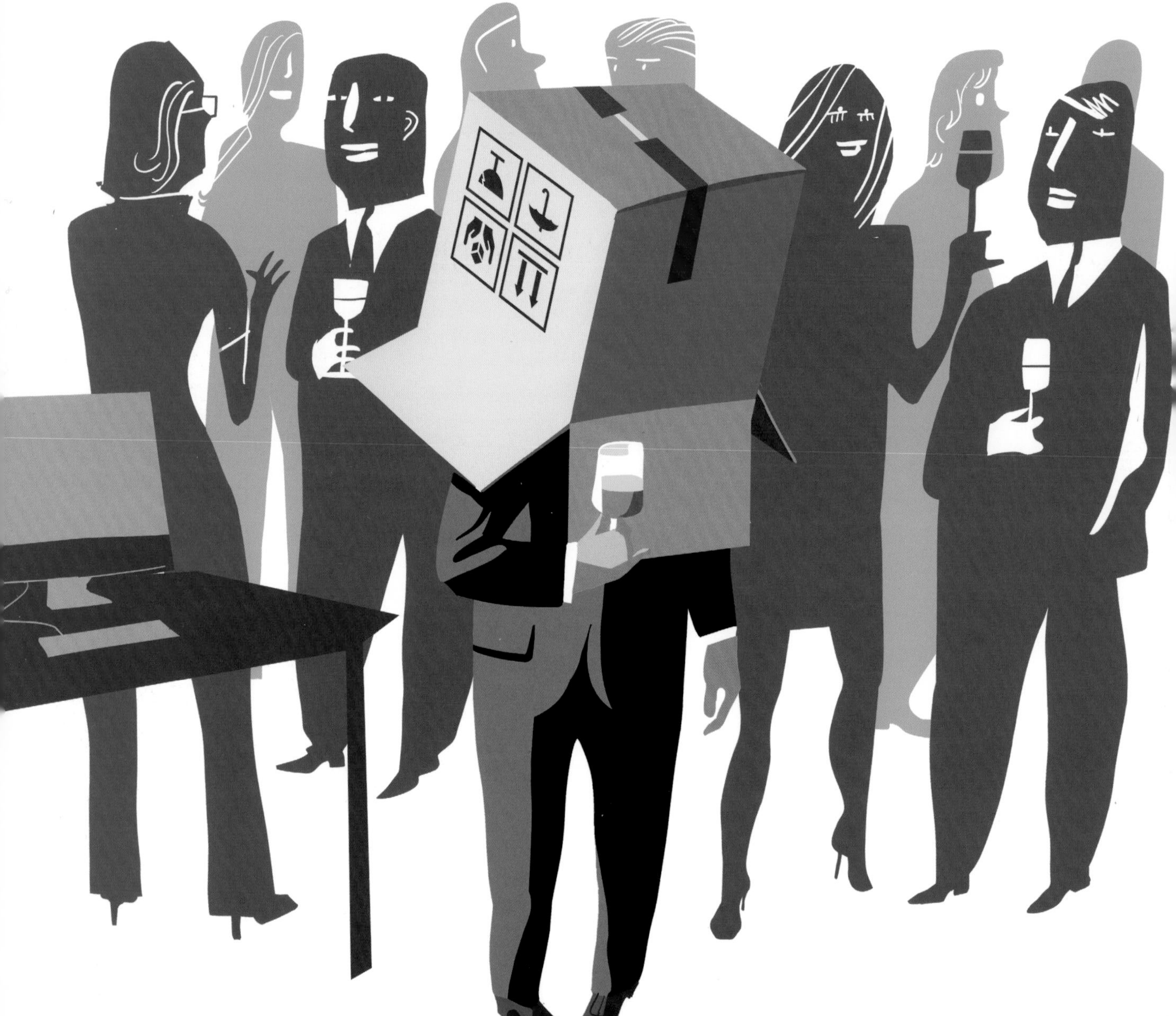

feeling nervous at a work apéro because it involves making small talk

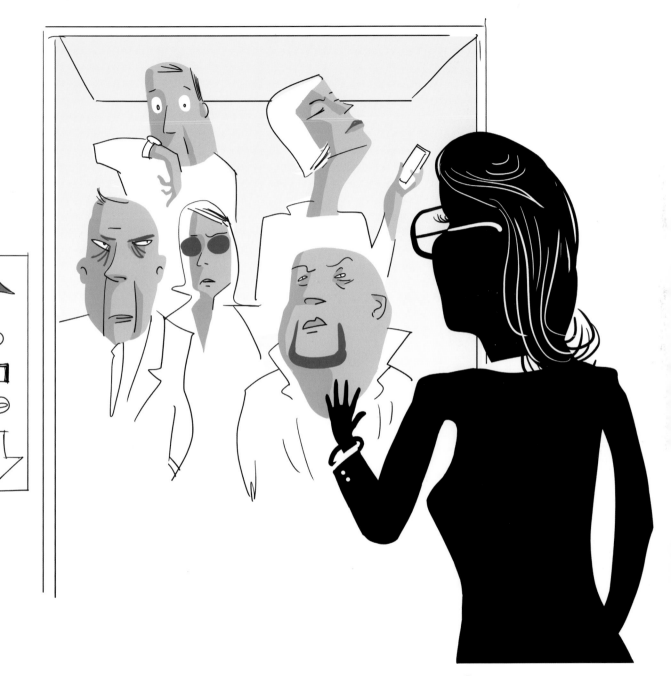

saying hello to everyone when entering a lift

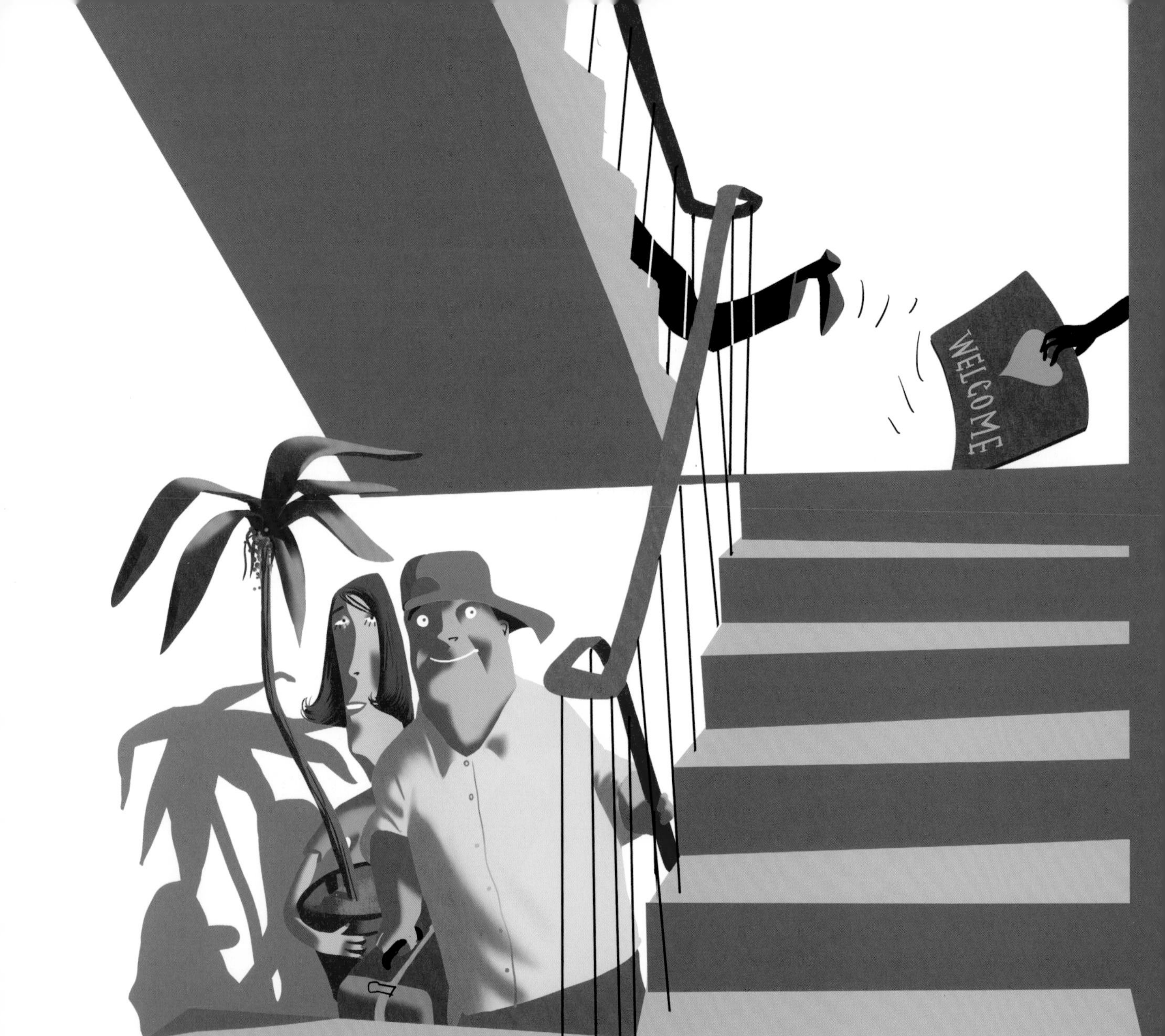
WELCOME

being nice and polite to your new neighbours

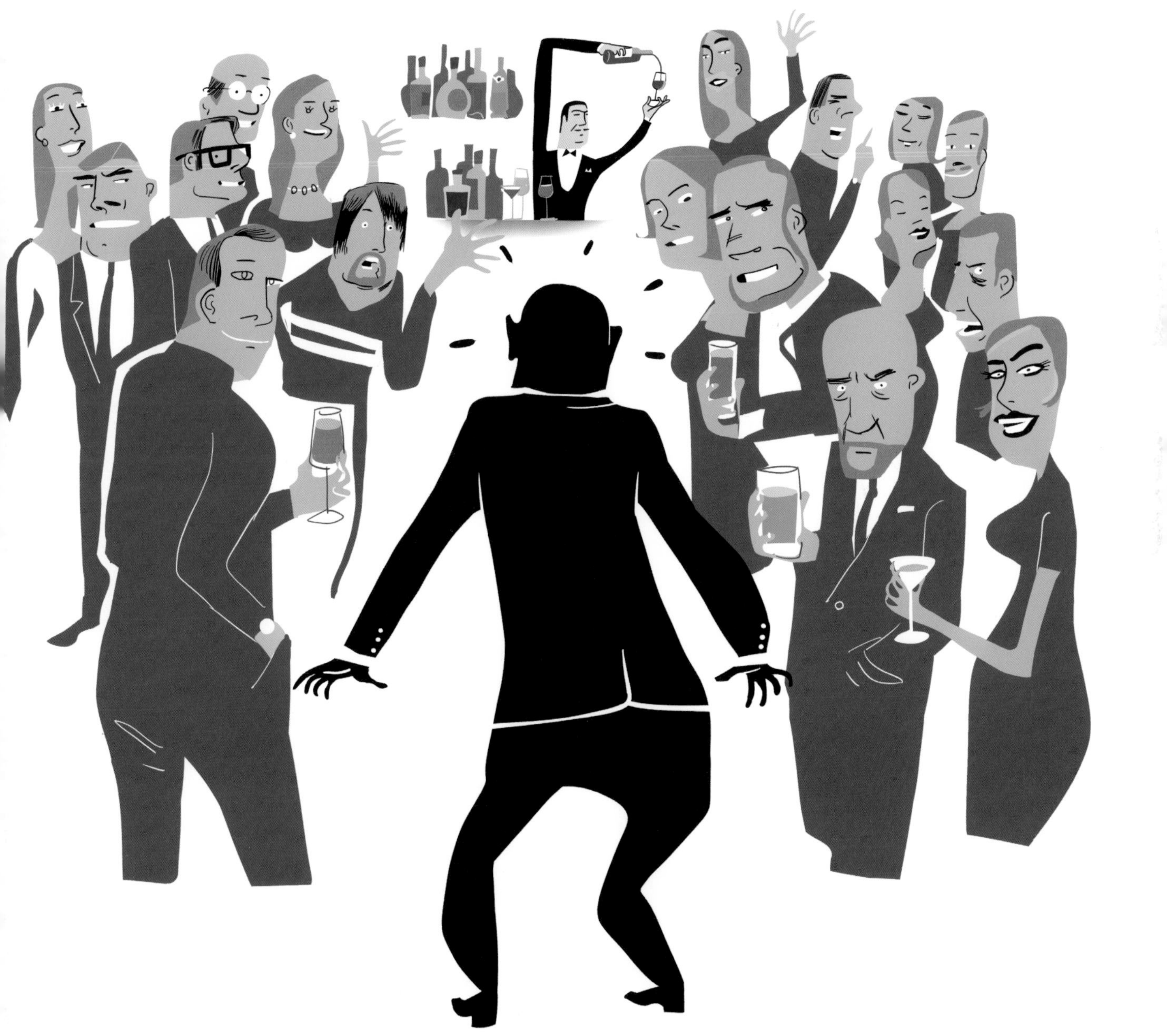

arriving last at a social event and having to introduce yourself to everyone before getting a drink

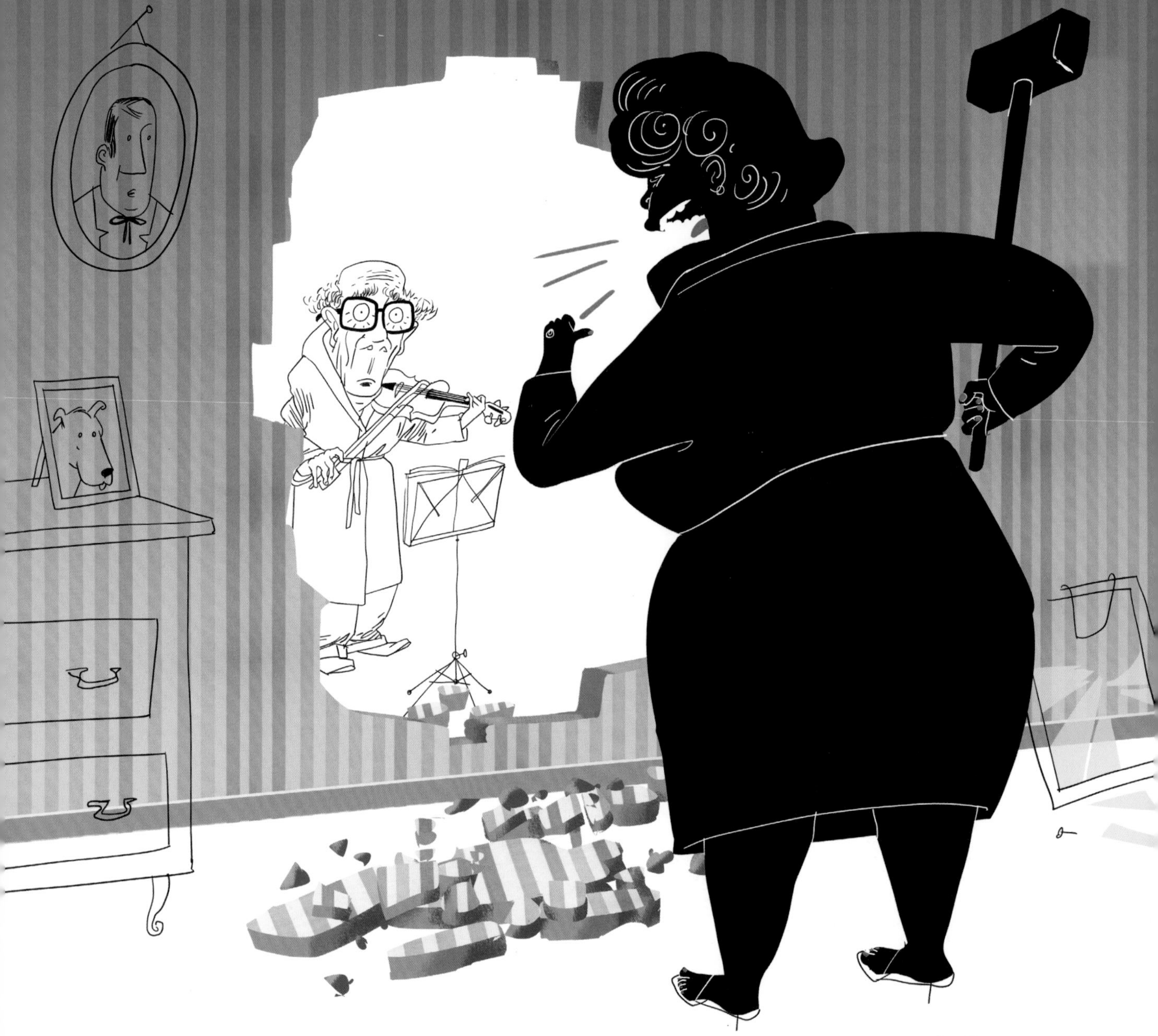

getting annoyed that your neighbour is being too loud at 10.30pm

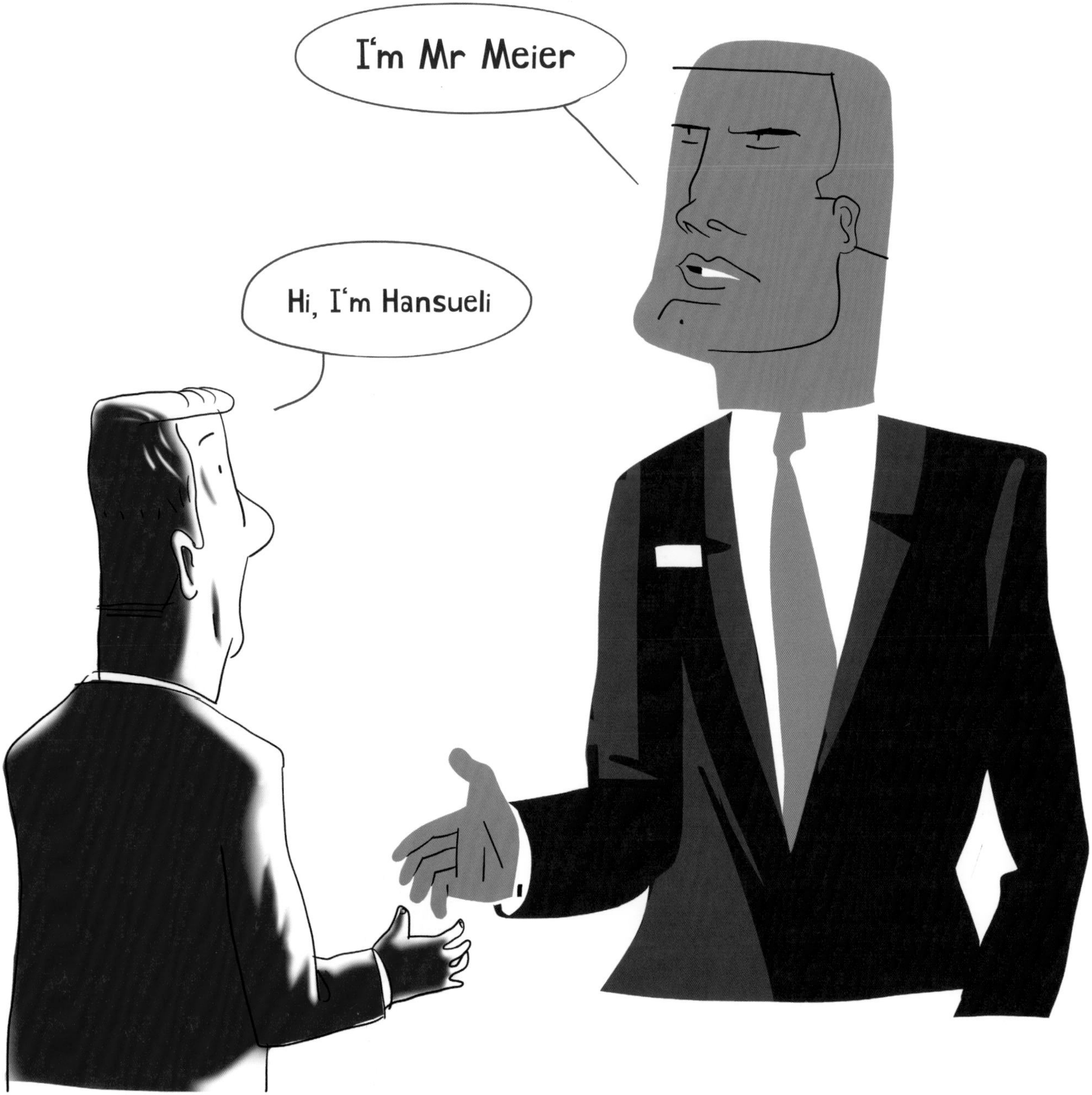
I'm Mr Meier
Hi, I'm Hansueli

having to use your boss's last name until
one of you retires

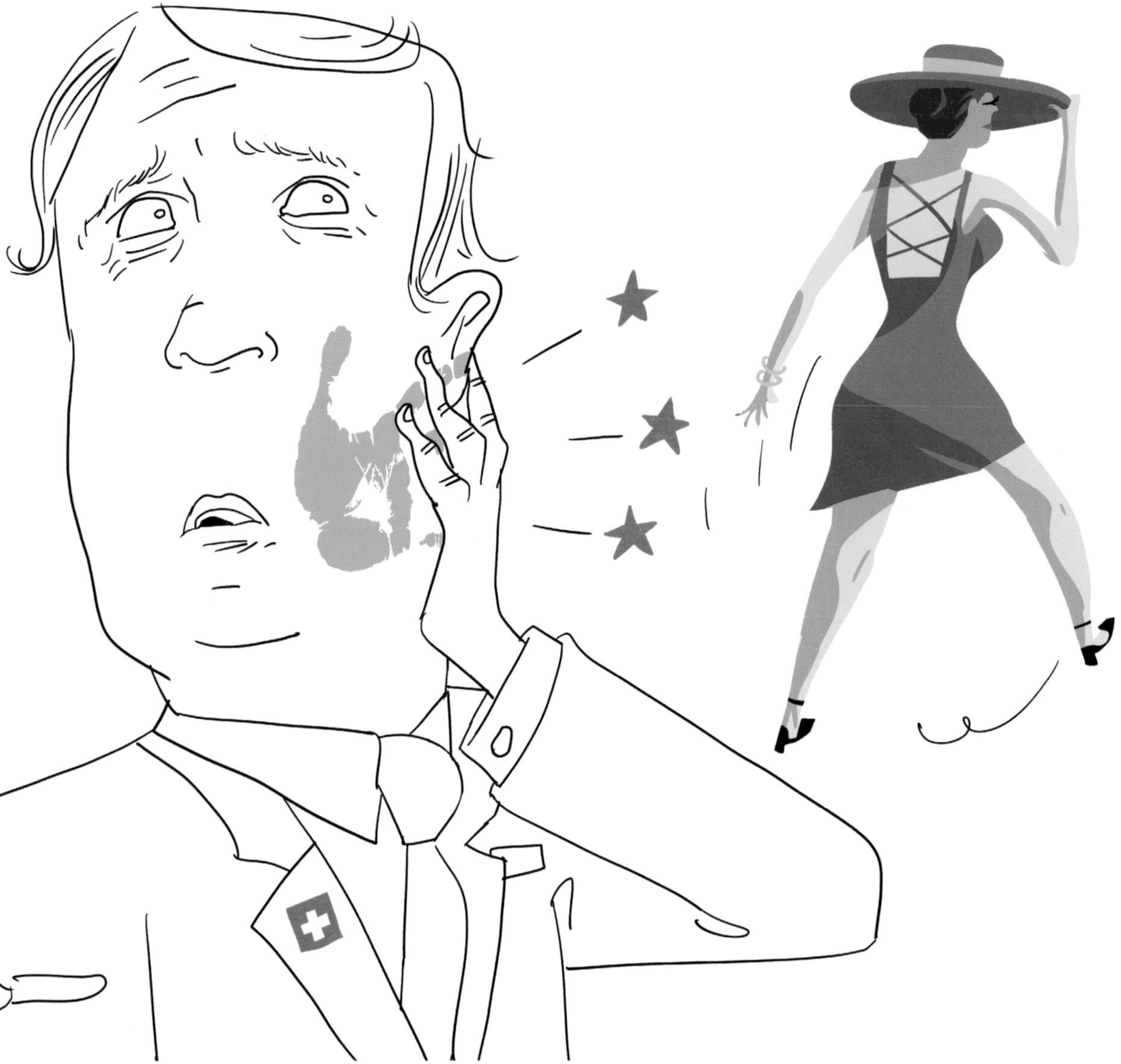

kissing hello three times even when abroad

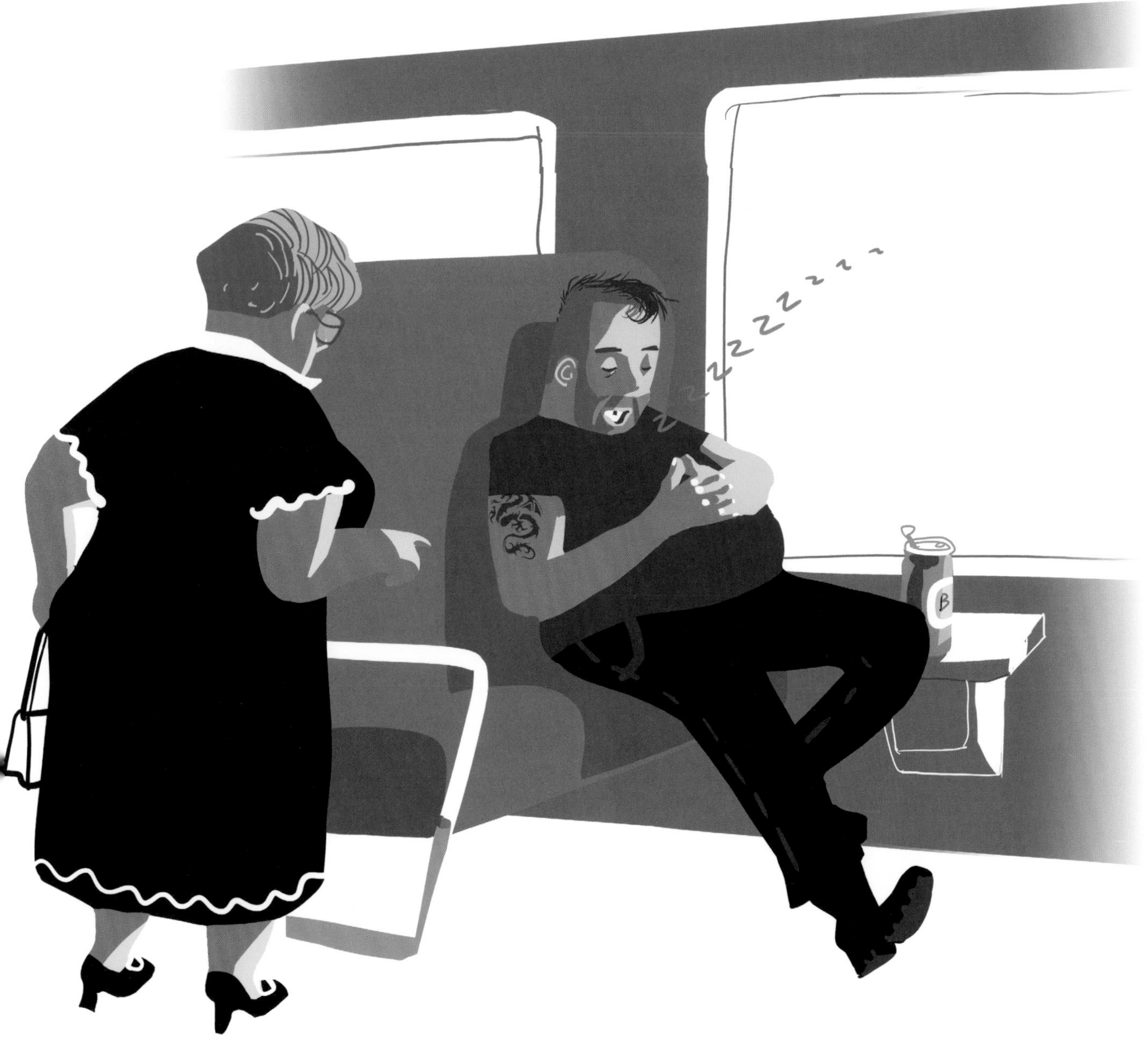
B

asking if an empty seat on the train is still free even when it clearly is

Step 2:
Swiss history you (almost) need to know
If the greatest events in Swiss history also included the ones that really mattered, this is how Switzerland's timeline would look.

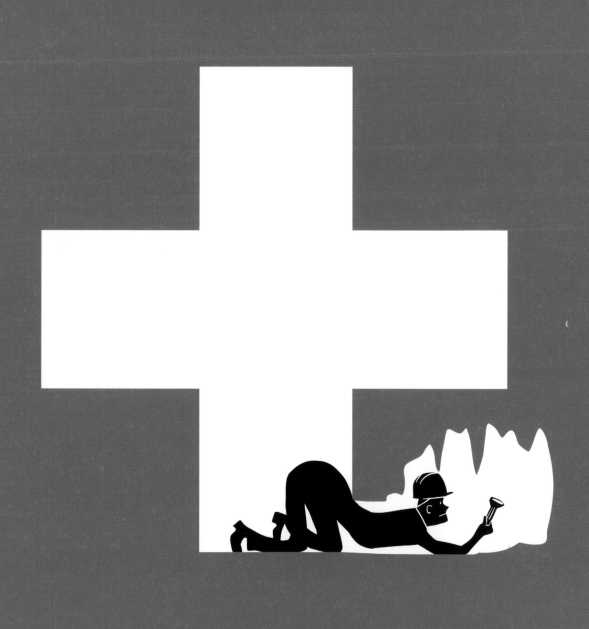

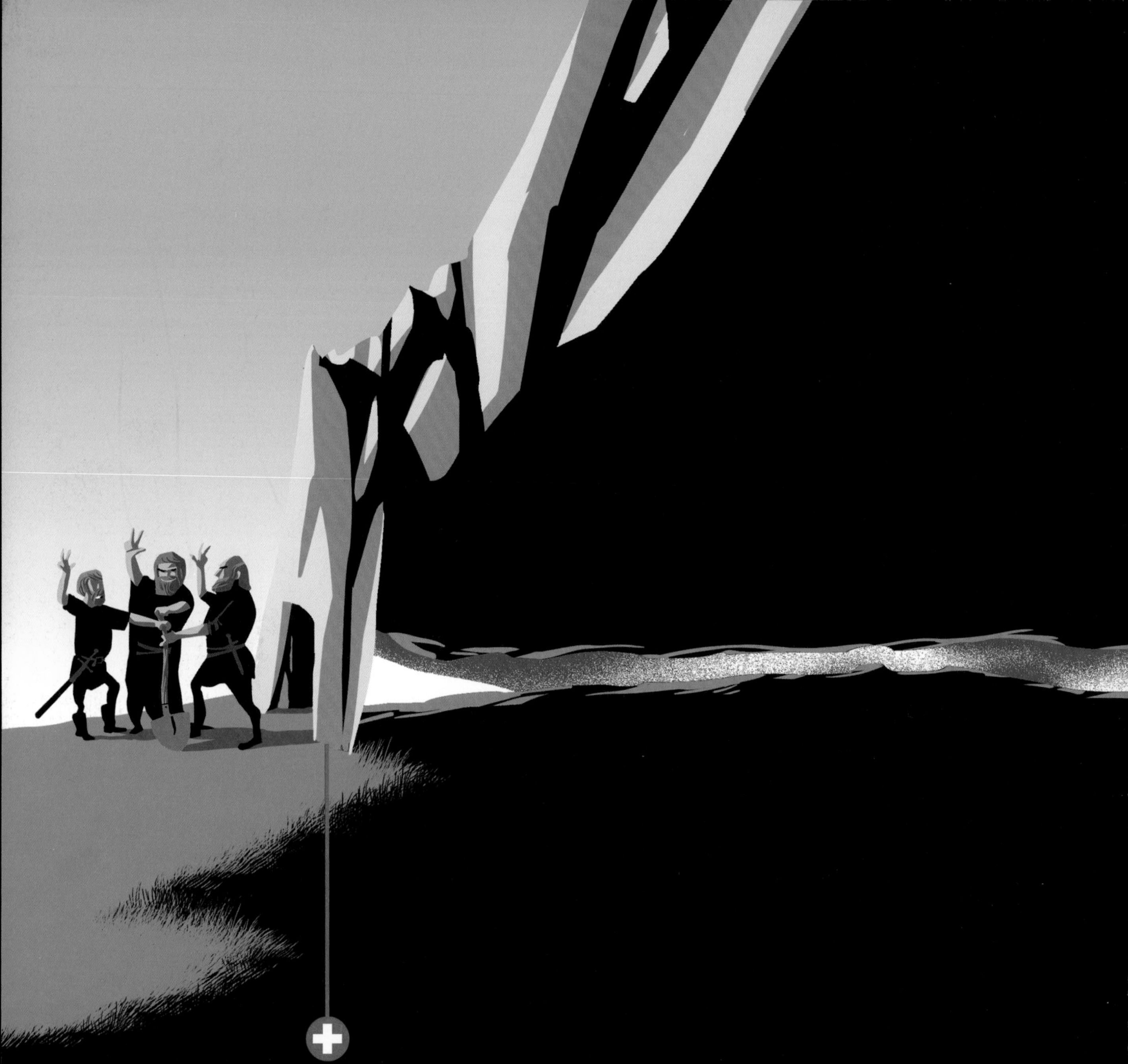

1291 Switzerland is founded by three men swearing to be best friends in Rütli meadow, at least that's how the story goes.

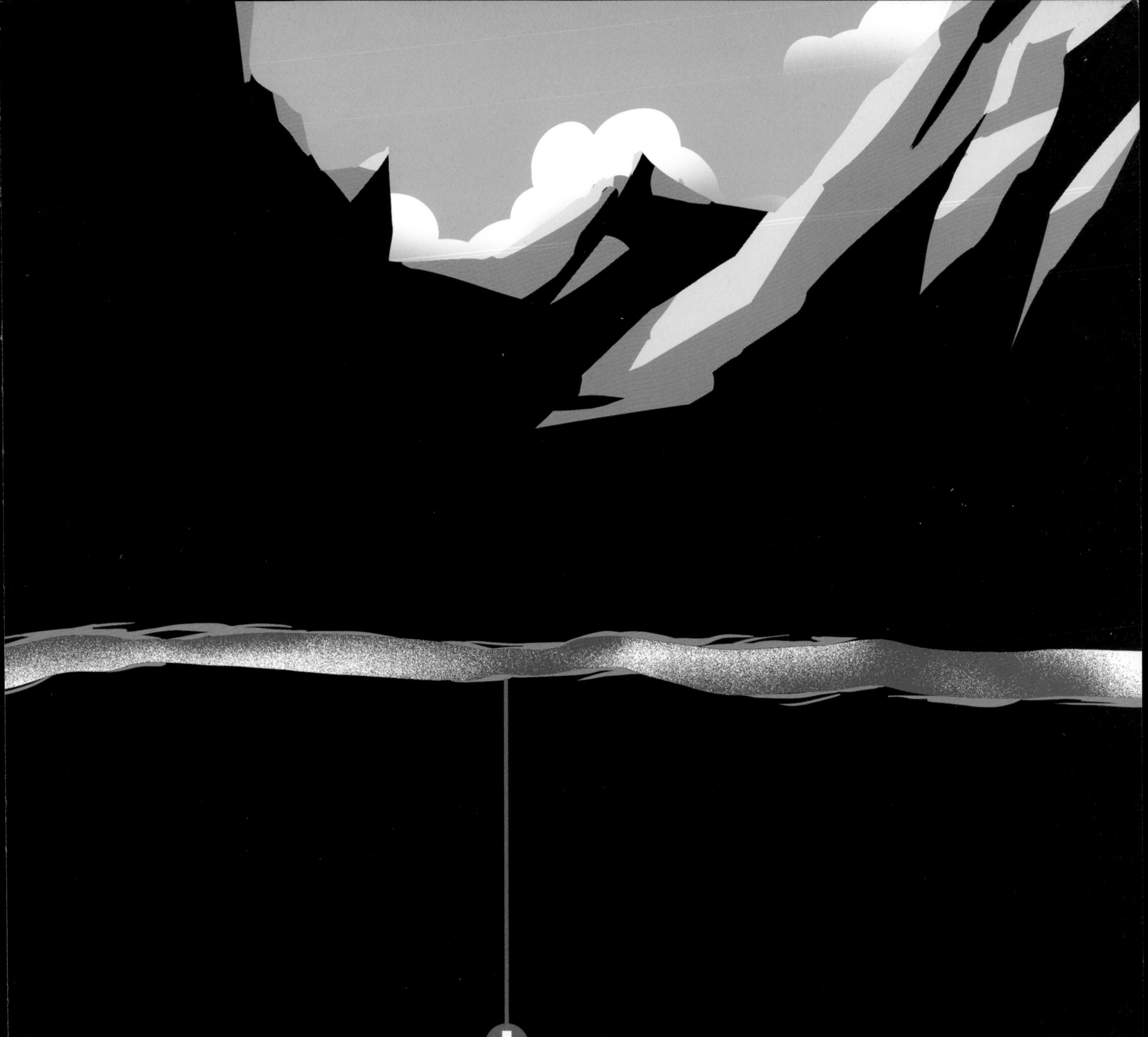

Nothing much happens

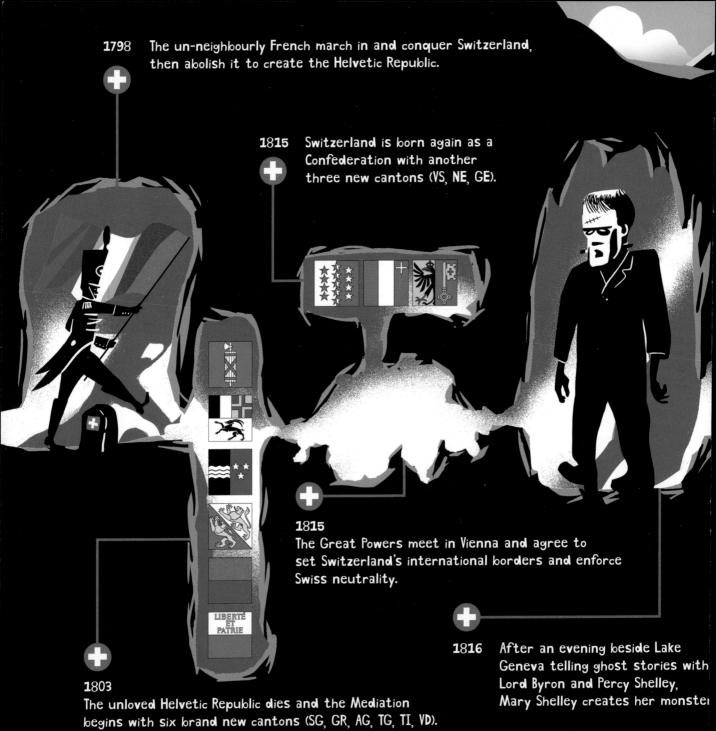

1798 The un-neighbourly French march in and conquer Switzerland, then abolish it to create the Helvetic Republic.

1815 Switzerland is born again as a Confederation with another three new cantons (VS, NE, GE).

1815
The Great Powers meet in Vienna and agree to set Switzerland's international borders and enforce Swiss neutrality.

1803
The unloved Helvetic Republic dies and the Mediation begins with six brand new cantons (SG, GR, AG, TG, TI, VD).

1816 After an evening beside Lake Geneva telling ghost stories with Lord Byron and Percy Shelley, Mary Shelley creates her monster

LIBERTÉ ET PATRIE

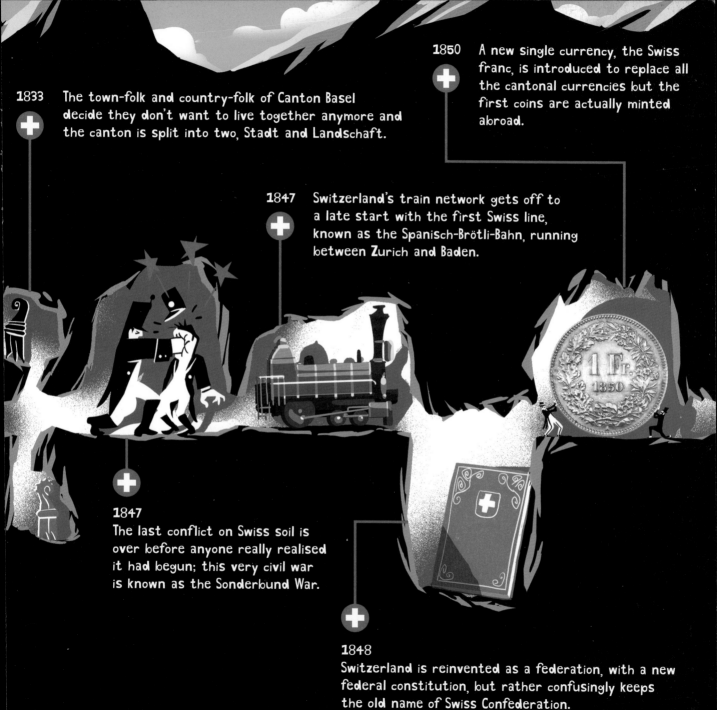

1833 The town-folk and country-folk of Canton Basel decide they don't want to live together anymore and the canton is split into two, Stadt and Landschaft.

1850 A new single currency, the Swiss franc, is introduced to replace all the cantonal currencies but the first coins are actually minted abroad.

1847 Switzerland's train network gets off to a late start with the first Swiss line, known as the Spanisch-Brötli-Bahn, running between Zurich and Baden.

1847
The last conflict on Swiss soil is over before anyone really realised it had begun; this very civil war is known as the Sonderbund War.

1848
Switzerland is reinvented as a federation, with a new federal constitution, but rather confusingly keeps the old name of Swiss Confederation.

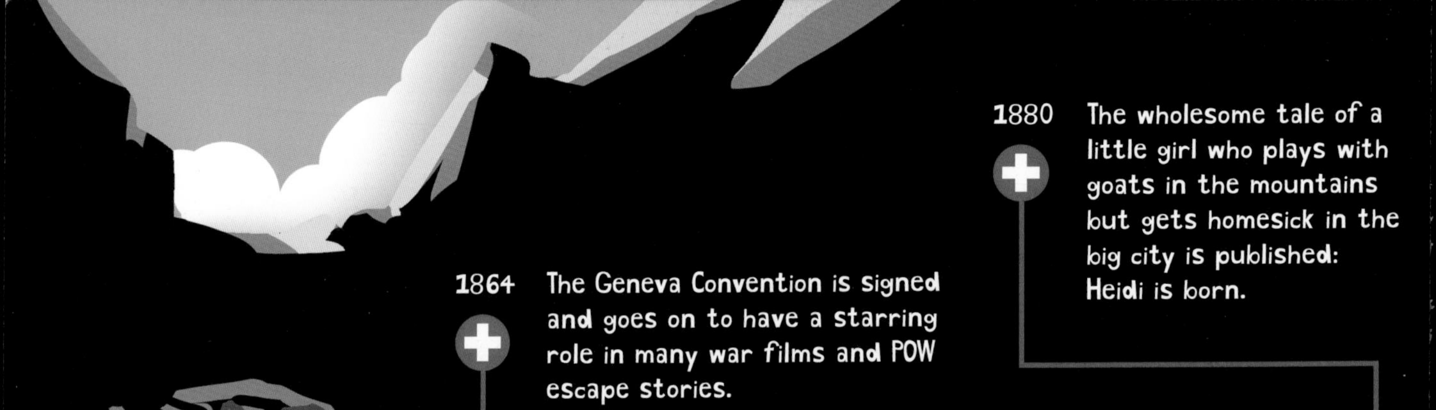

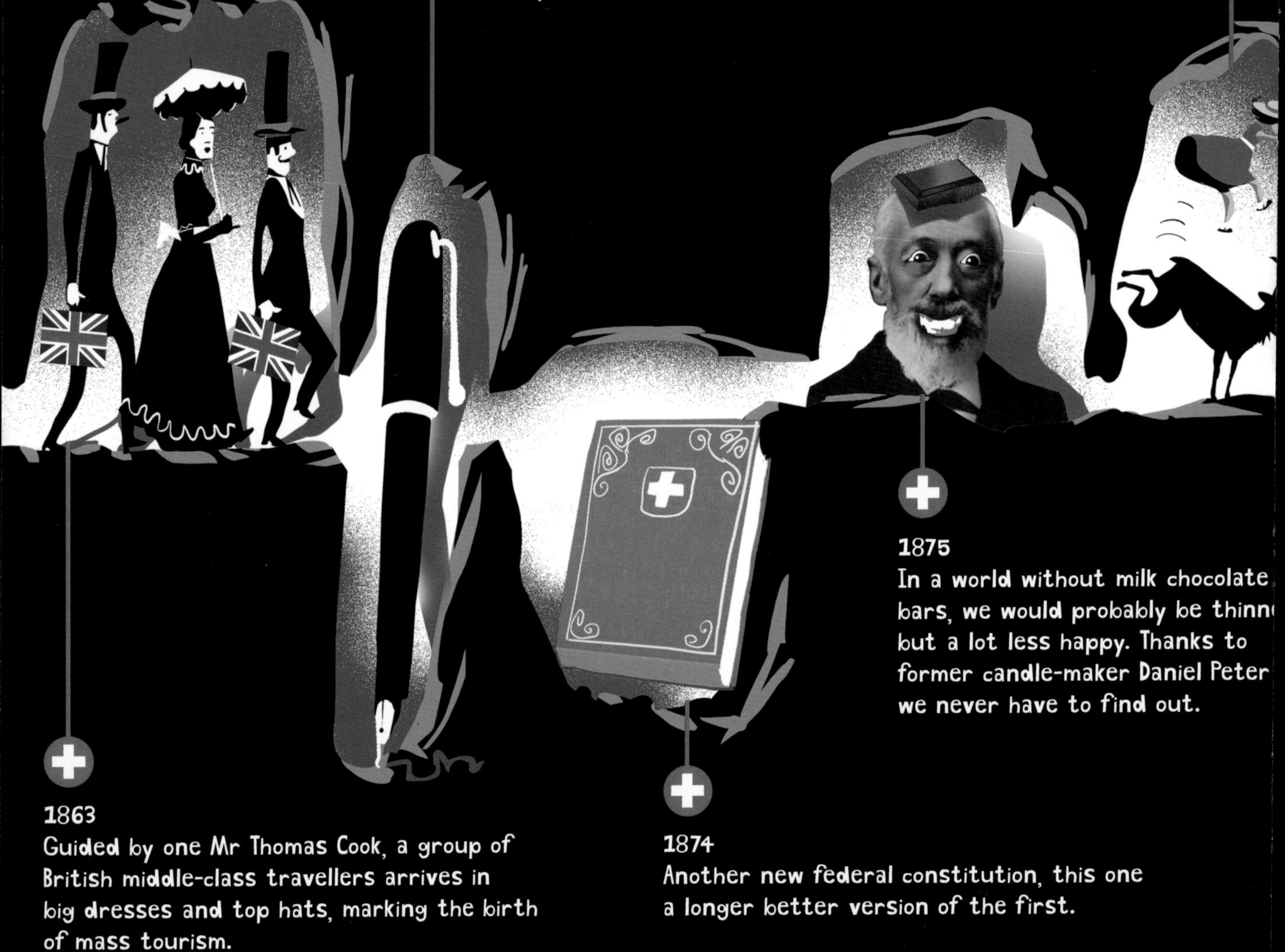

1863
Guided by one Mr Thomas Cook, a group of British middle-class travellers arrives in big dresses and top hats, marking the birth of mass tourism.

1864 The Geneva Convention is signed and goes on to have a starring role in many war films and POW escape stories.

1874
Another new federal constitution, this one a longer better version of the first.

1875
In a world without milk chocolate bars, we would probably be thinn but a lot less happy. Thanks to former candle-maker Daniel Peter we never have to find out.

1880 The wholesome tale of a little girl who plays with goats in the mountains but gets homesick in the big city is published: Heidi is born.

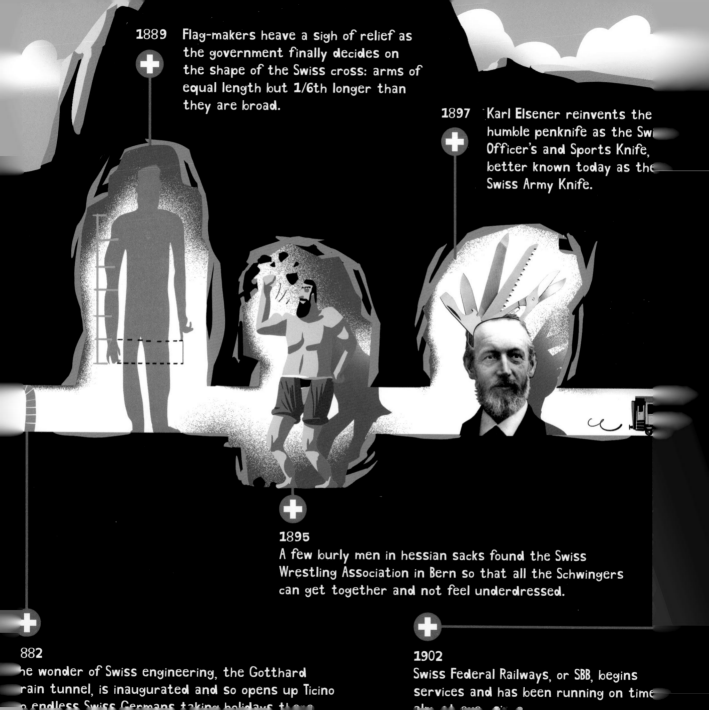

1889 Flag-makers heave a sigh of relief as the government finally decides on the shape of the Swiss cross: arms of equal length but 1/6th longer than they are broad.

1897 Karl Elsener reinvents the humble penknife as the Sw[i] Officer's and Sports Knife, better known today as the Swiss Army Knife.

1895
A few burly men in hessian sacks found the Swiss Wrestling Association in Bern so that all the Schwingers can get together and not feel underdressed.

882
he wonder of Swiss engineering, the Gotthard
rain tunnel, is inaugurated and so opens up Ticino
o endless Swiss Germans taking holidays there

1902
Swiss Federal Railways, or SBB, begins services and has been running on time

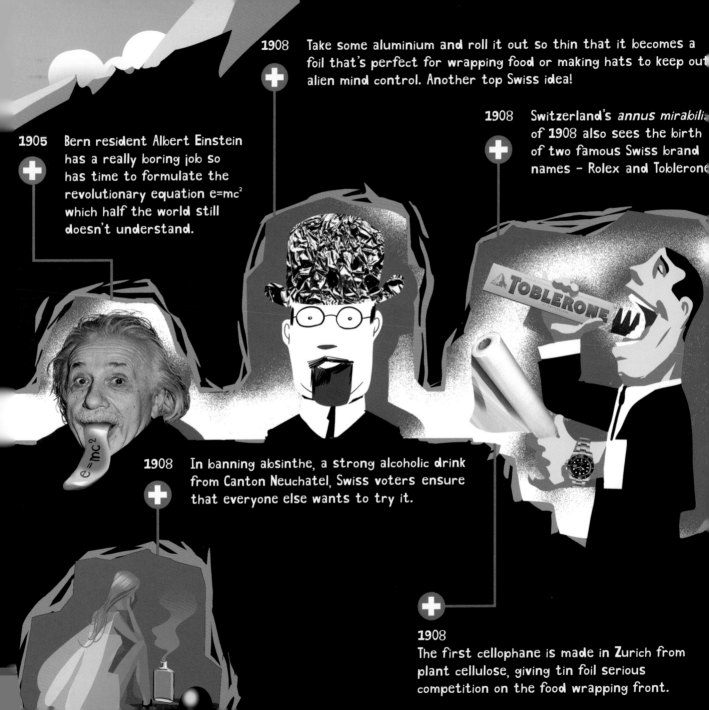

1908 Take some aluminium and roll it out so thin that it becomes a foil that's perfect for wrapping food or making hats to keep out alien mind control. Another top Swiss idea!

1908 Switzerland's *annus mirabili* of 1908 also sees the birth of two famous Swiss brand names – Rolex and Toblerone

1905 Bern resident Albert Einstein has a really boring job so has time to formulate the revolutionary equation e=mc² which half the world still doesn't understand.

1908 In banning absinthe, a strong alcoholic drink from Canton Neuchatel, Swiss voters ensure that everyone else wants to try it.

1908
The first cellophane is made in Zurich from plant cellulose, giving tin foil serious competition on the food wrapping front.

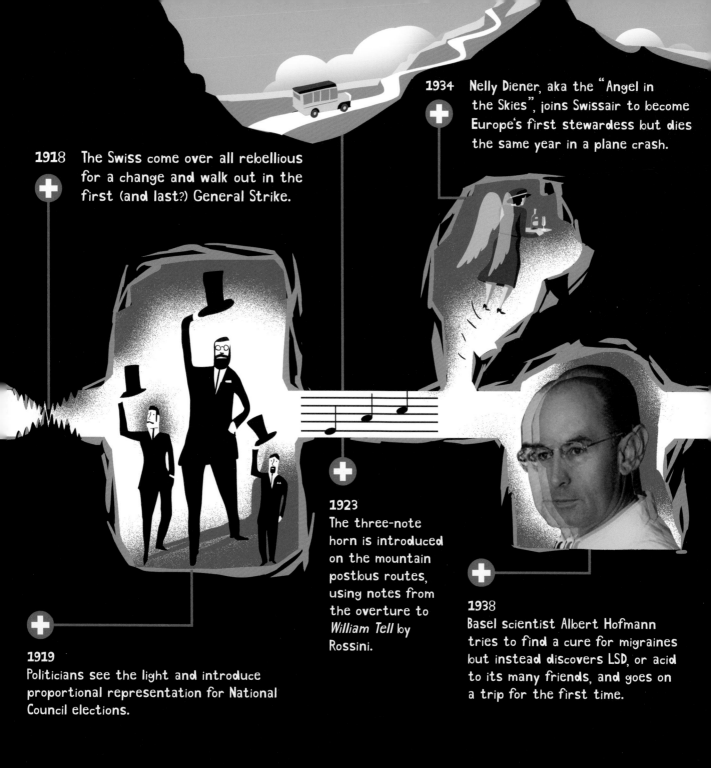

1918 The Swiss come over all rebellious for a change and walk out in the first (and last?) General Strike.

1934 Nelly Diener, aka the "Angel in the Skies", joins Swissair to become Europe's first stewardess but dies the same year in a plane crash.

1923
The three-note horn is introduced on the mountain postbus routes, using notes from the overture to *William Tell* by Rossini.

1919
Politicians see the light and introduce proportional representation for National Council elections.

1938
Basel scientist Albert Hofmann tries to find a cure for migraines but instead discovers LSD, or acid to its many friends, and goes on a trip for the first time.

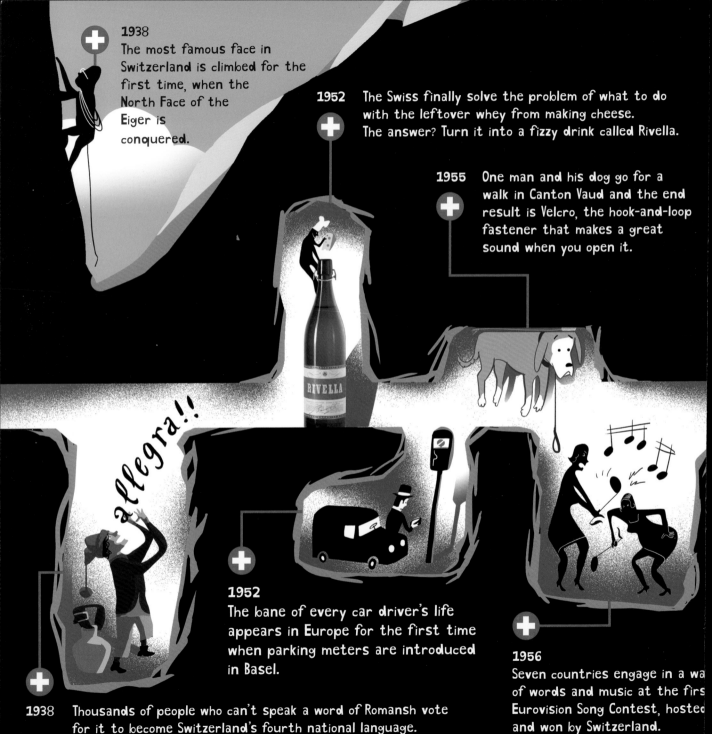

1938 The most famous face in Switzerland is climbed for the first time, when the North Face of the Eiger is conquered.

1952 The Swiss finally solve the problem of what to do with the leftover whey from making cheese. The answer? Turn it into a fizzy drink called Rivella.

1955 One man and his dog go for a walk in Canton Vaud and the end result is Velcro, the hook-and-loop fastener that makes a great sound when you open it.

allegra!!

RIVELLA

1952 The bane of every car driver's life appears in Europe for the first time when parking meters are introduced in Basel.

1956 Seven countries engage in a war of words and music at the first Eurovision Song Contest, hosted and won by Switzerland.

1938 Thousands of people who can't speak a word of Romansh vote for it to become Switzerland's fourth national language.

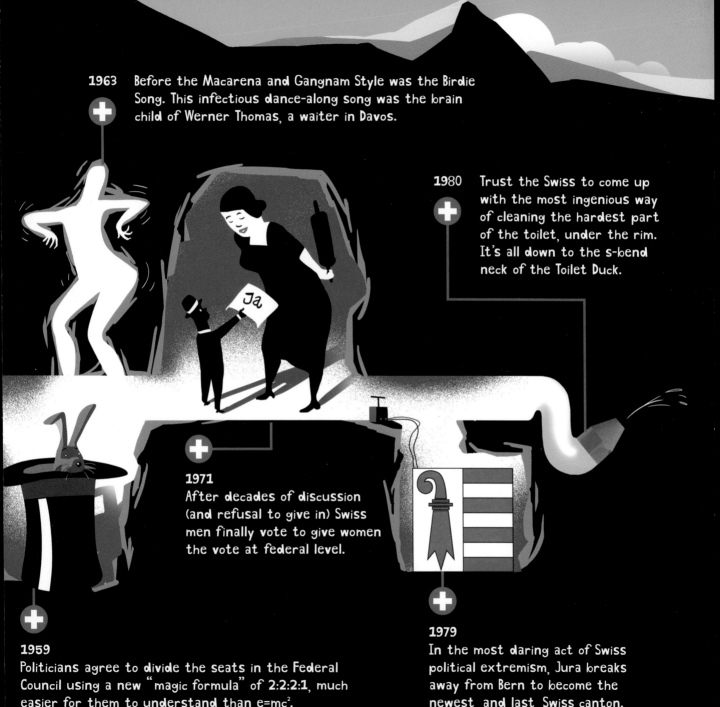

1963 Before the Macarena and Gangnam Style was the Birdie Song. This infectious dance-along song was the brain child of Werner Thomas, a waiter in Davos.

1980 Trust the Swiss to come up with the most ingenious way of cleaning the hardest part of the toilet, under the rim. It's all down to the s-bend neck of the Toilet Duck.

Ja

1971
After decades of discussion (and refusal to give in) Swiss men finally vote to give women the vote at federal level.

1959
Politicians agree to divide the seats in the Federal Council using a new "magic formula" of 2:2:2:1, much easier for them to understand than e=mc².

1979
In the most daring act of Swiss political extremism, Jura breaks away from Bern to become the newest and last Swiss canton.

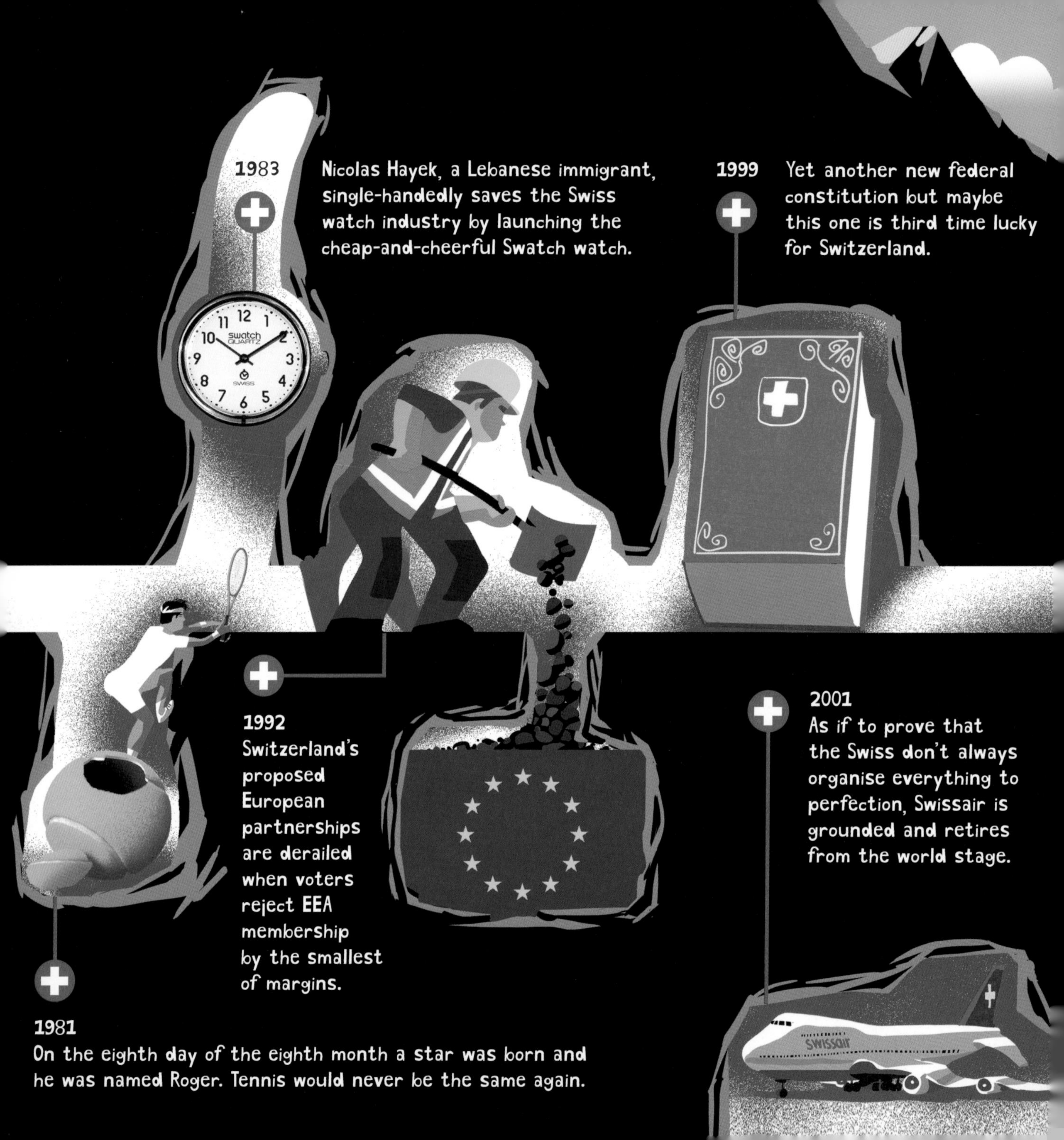
swatch
QUARTZ
SWISS
swissair

1983 Nicolas Hayek, a Lebanese immigrant, single-handedly saves the Swiss watch industry by launching the cheap-and-cheerful Swatch watch.

1999 Yet another new federal constitution but maybe this one is third time lucky for Switzerland.

1992
Switzerland's proposed European partnerships are derailed when voters reject EEA membership by the smallest of margins.

2001
As if to prove that the Swiss don't always organise everything to perfection, Swissair is grounded and retires from the world stage.

1981
On the eighth day of the eighth month a star was born and he was named Roger. Tennis would never be the same again.

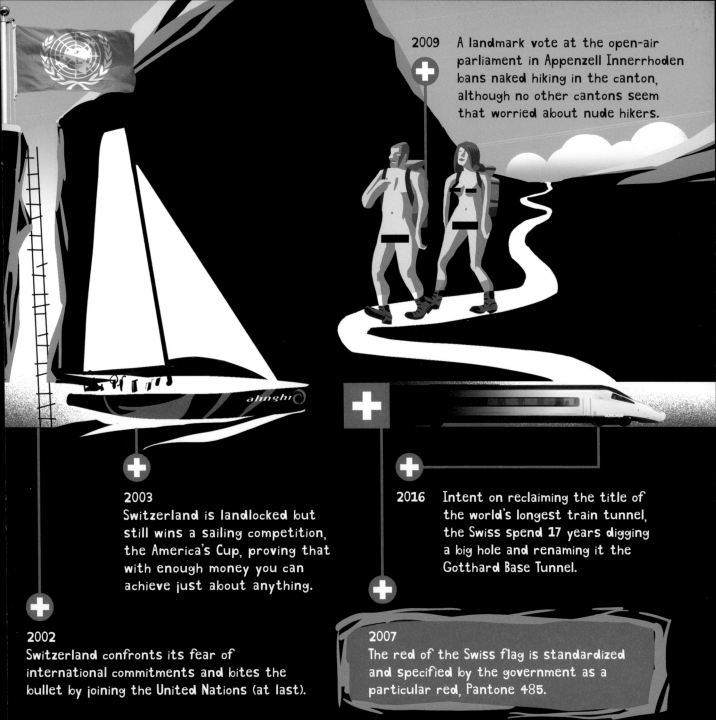

2009 A landmark vote at the open-air parliament in Appenzell Innerrhoden bans naked hiking in the canton, although no other cantons seem that worried about nude hikers.

2003
Switzerland is landlocked but still wins a sailing competition, the America's Cup, proving that with enough money you can achieve just about anything.

2016 Intent on reclaiming the title of the world's longest train tunnel, the Swiss spend **17** years digging a big hole and renaming it the Gotthard Base Tunnel.

2002
Switzerland confronts its fear of international commitments and bites the bullet by joining the United Nations (at last).

2007
The red of the Swiss flag is standardized and specified by the government as a particular red, Pantone 485.

Step 3:
Living like the Swiss
Those moments when you confront the reality of life in a totally Swiss environment, with rules governing everything.

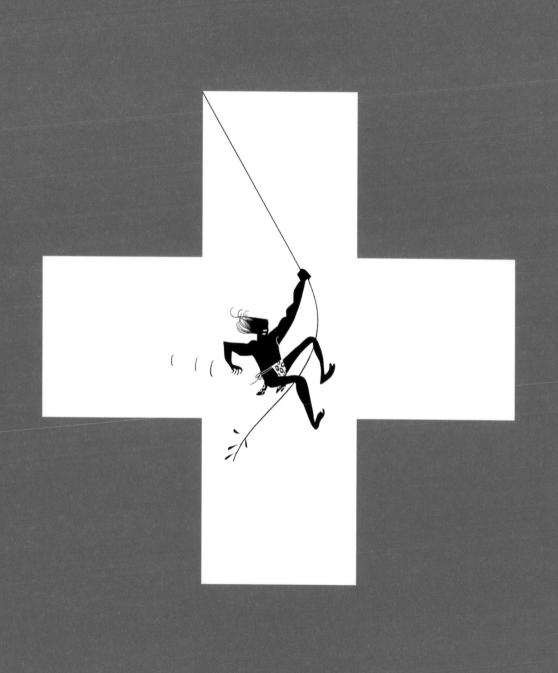

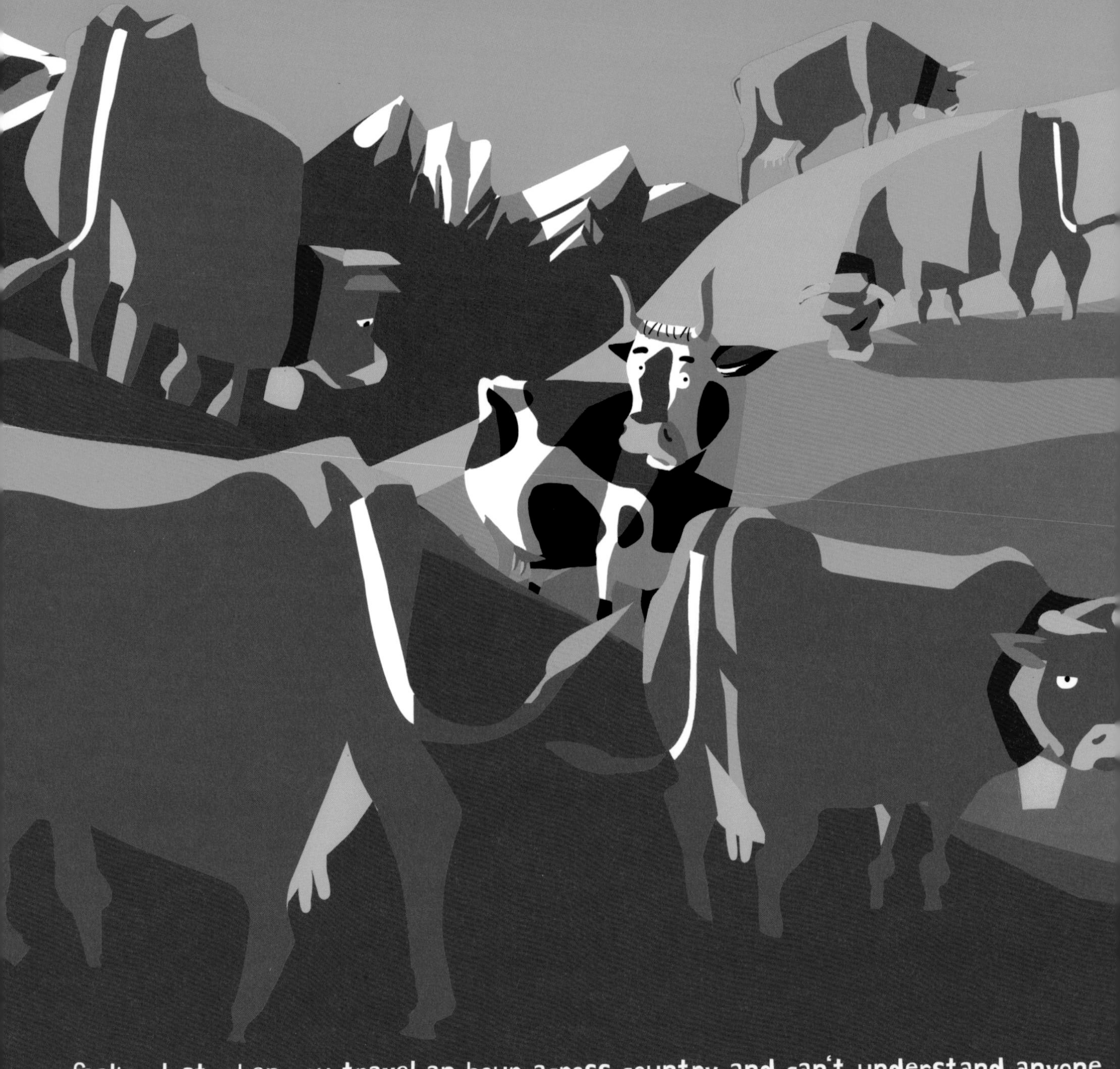

feeling lost when you travel an hour across country and can't understand anyone

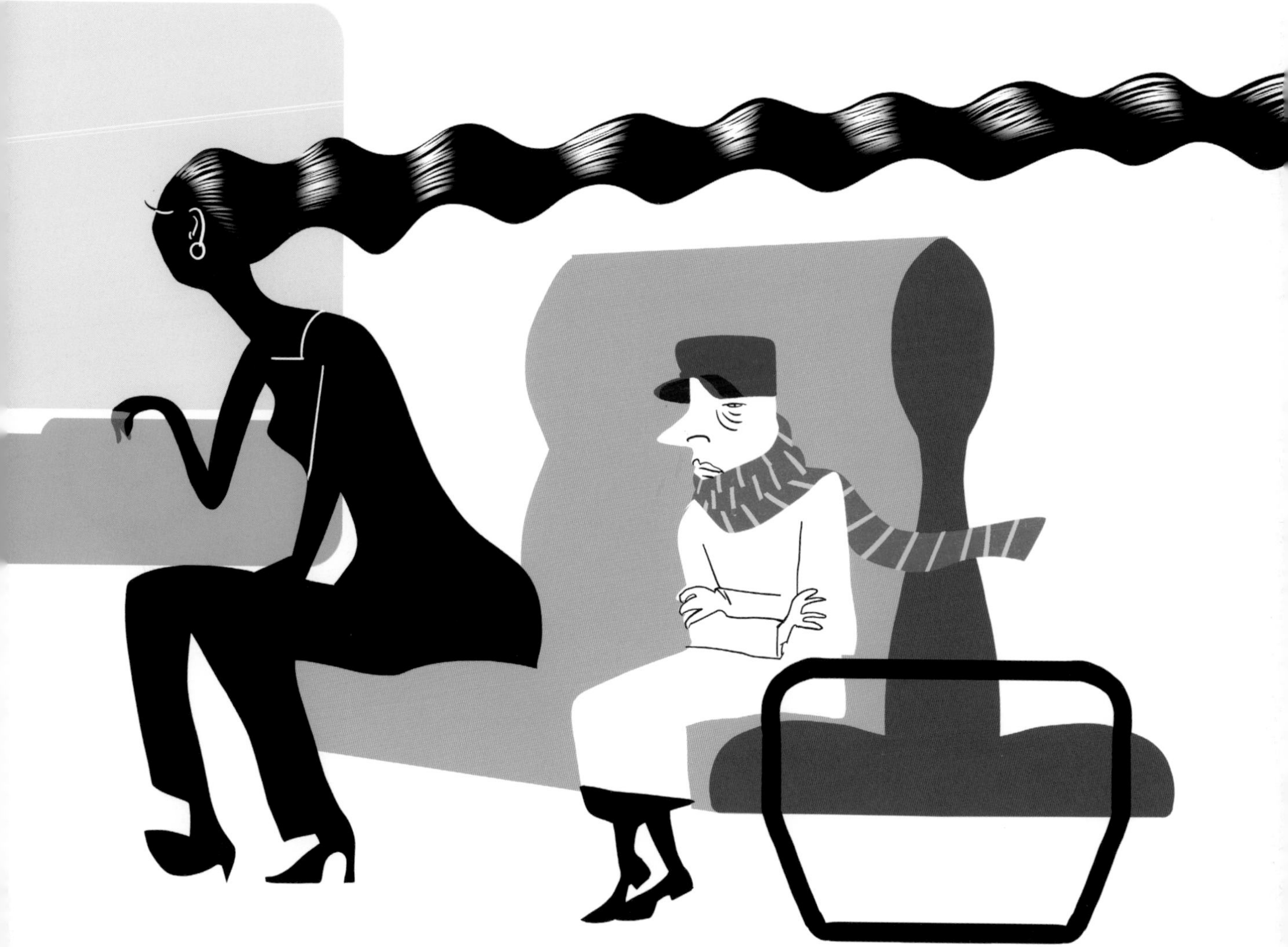

thinking that you'll get sick from a draught through an open window

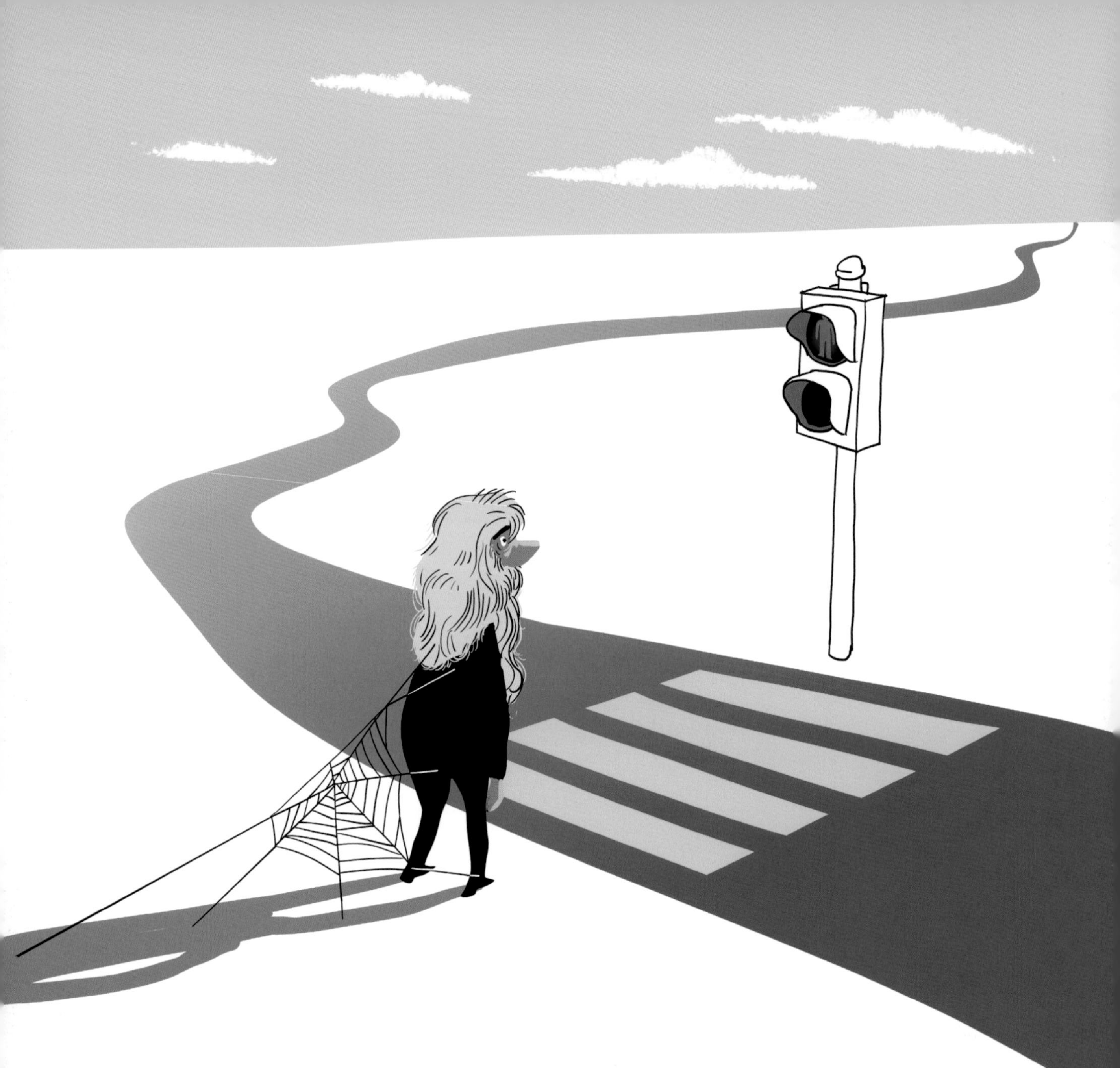

waiting to cross an empty street because the red man is still there

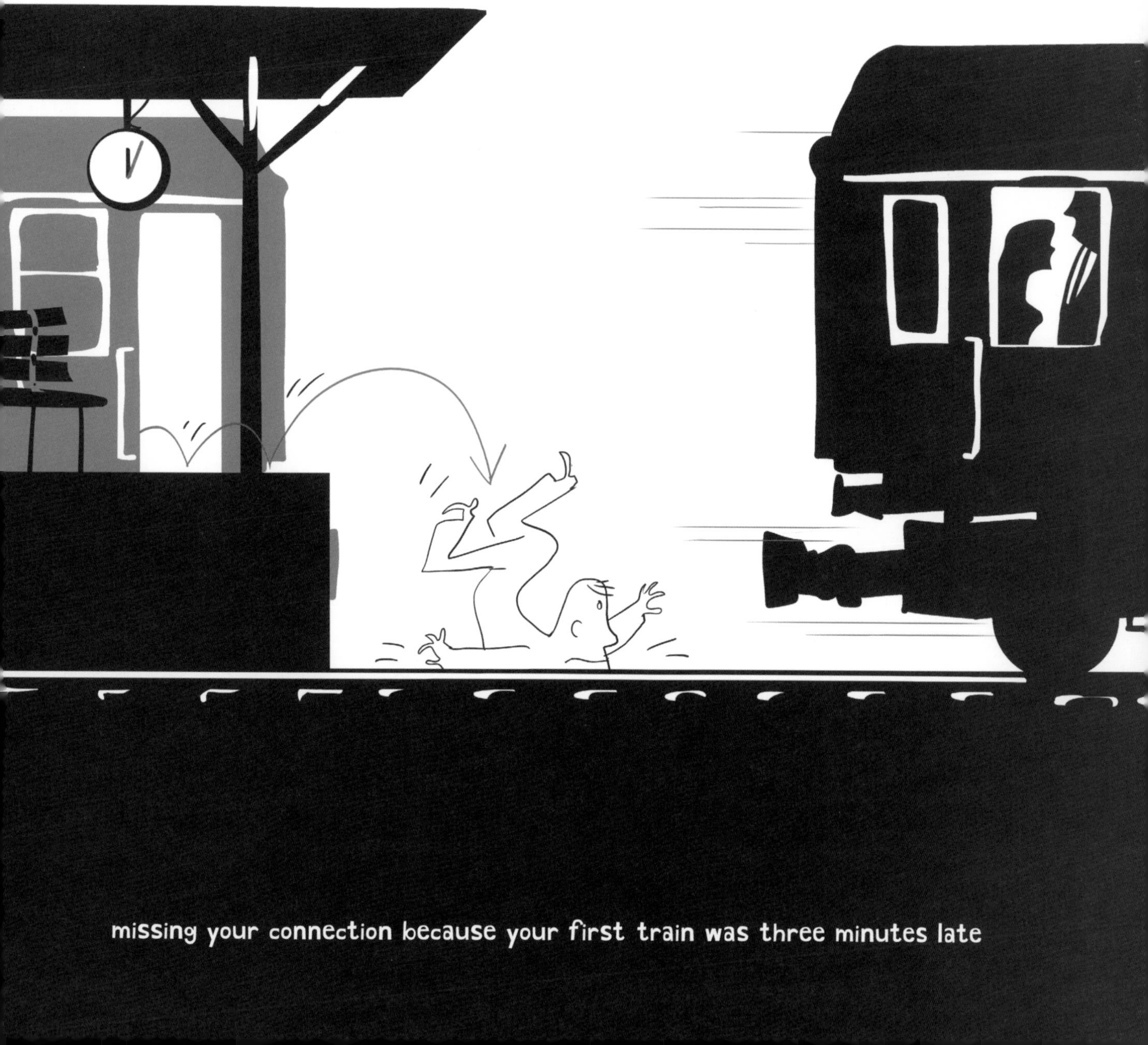

missing your connection because your first train was three minutes late

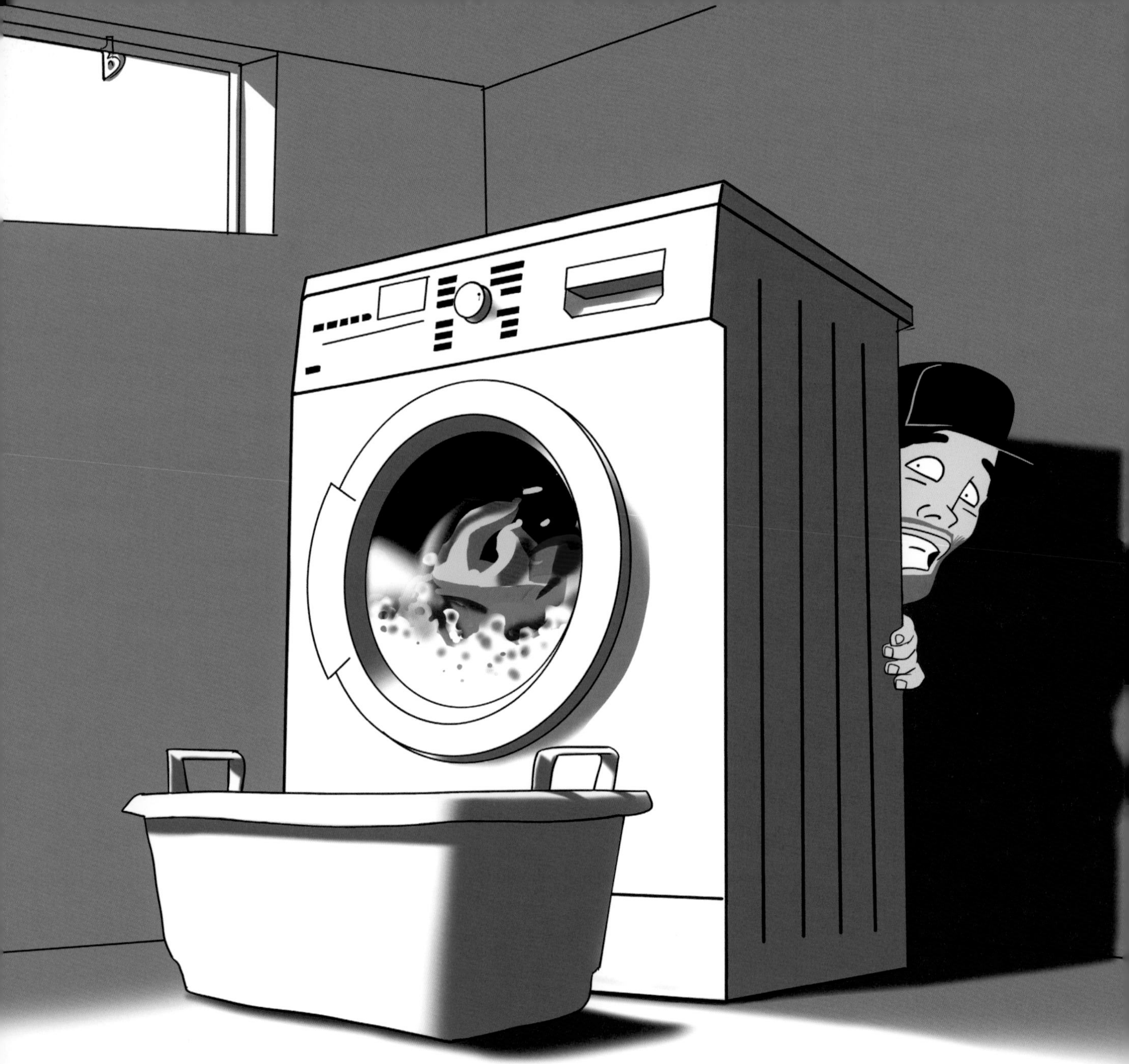

secretly doing your laundry even though it's not your designated day in the laundry room

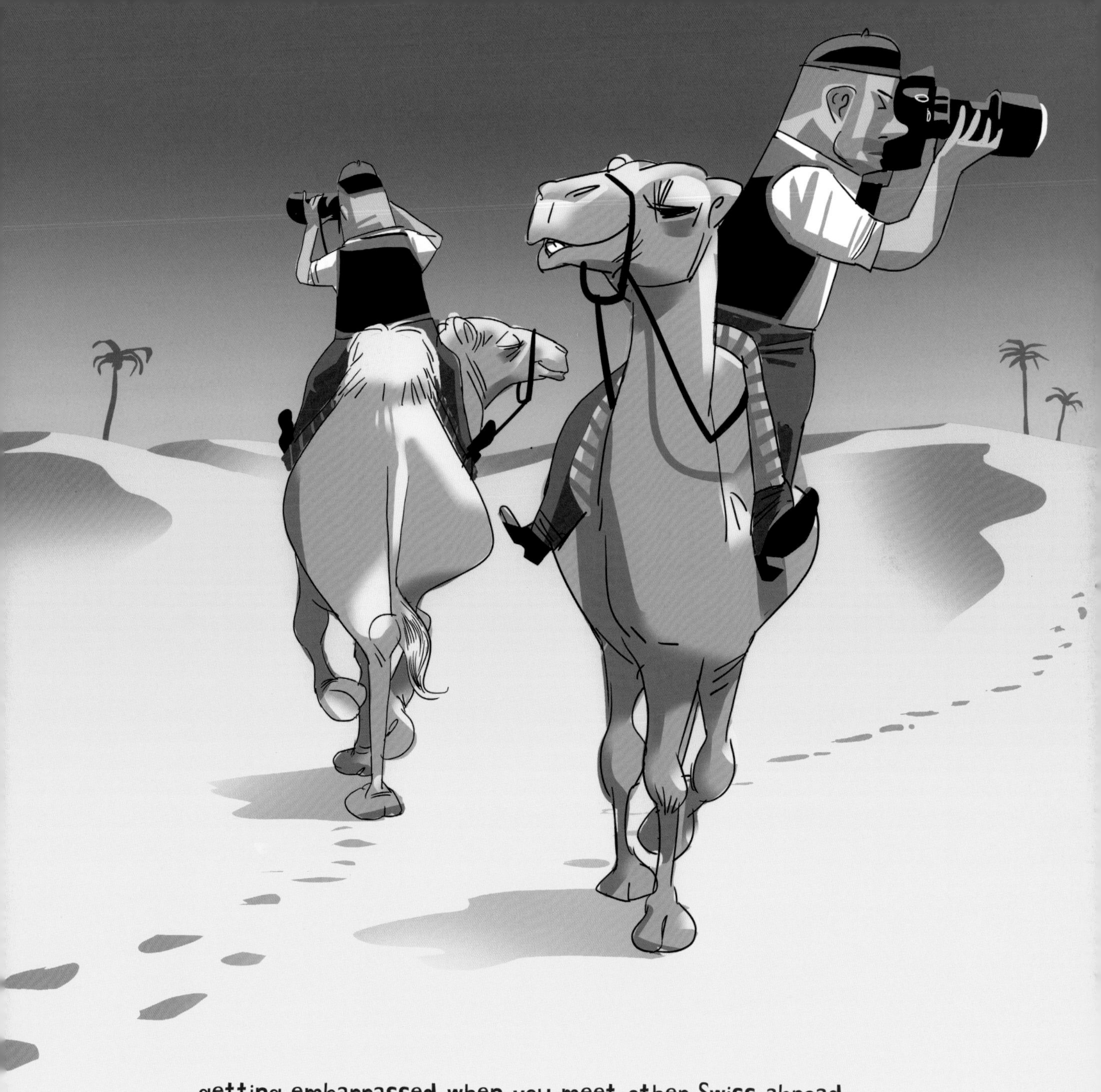

getting embarrassed when you meet other Swiss abroad

12

↓

Step 4:
The Swiss Commandments

If God were in fact a heavenly Helvetia, these are the twelve commandments that she would have us all live – and die – by.

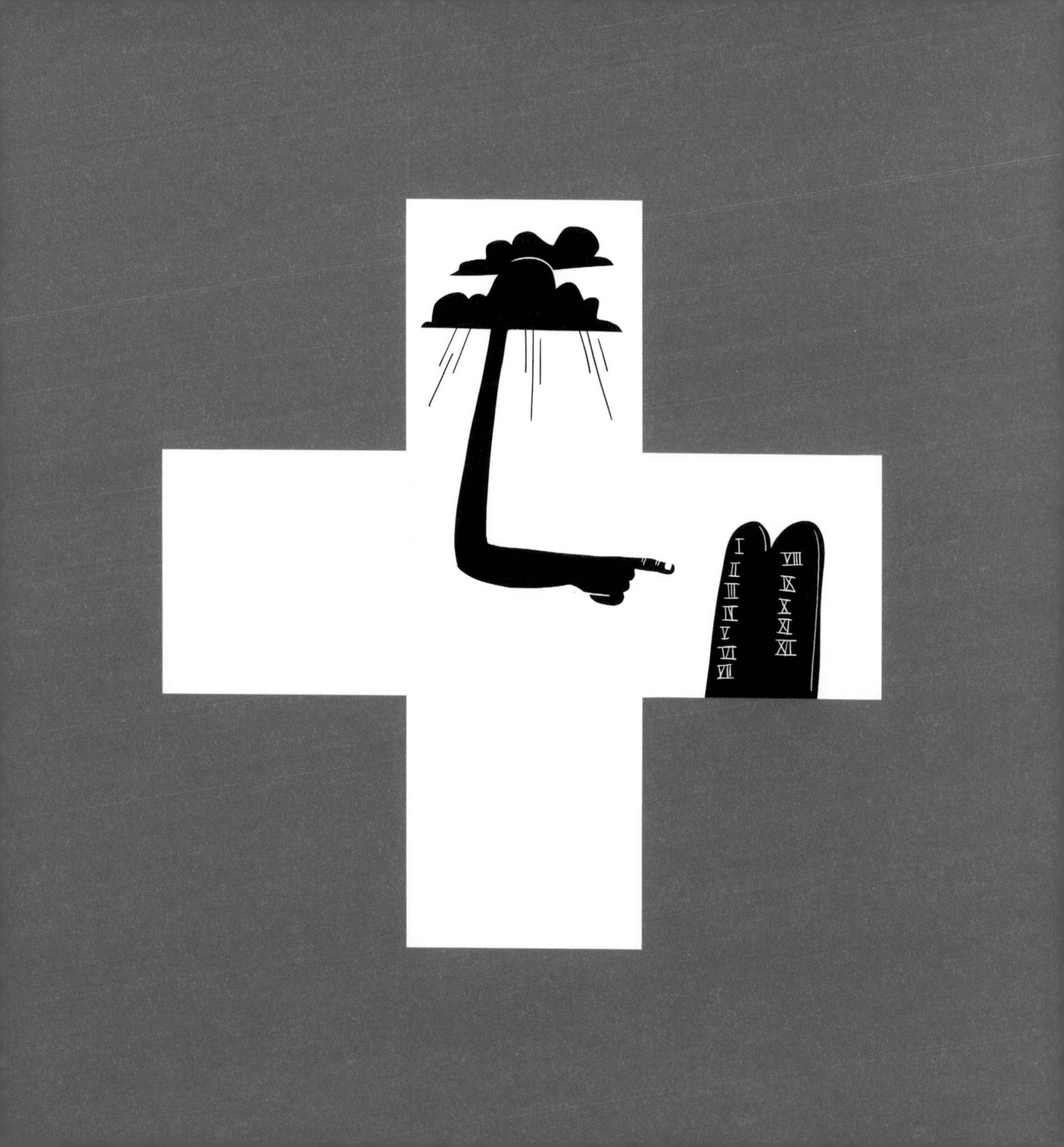

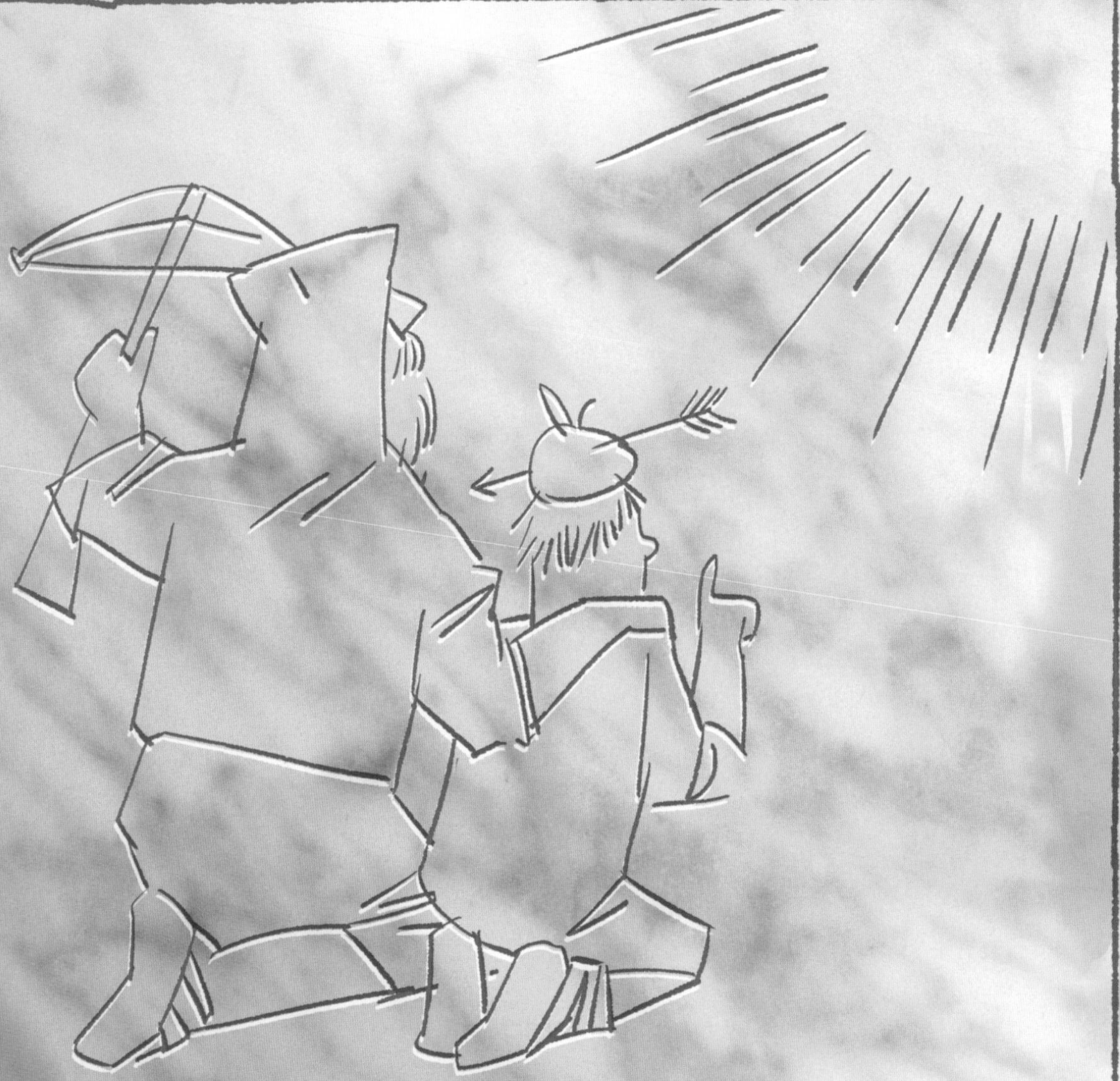

THE FIRST COMMANDMENT:
THOU SHALT BELIEVE IN WILLIAM TELL
AS THE ONE TRUE FOUNDER OF THY NATION

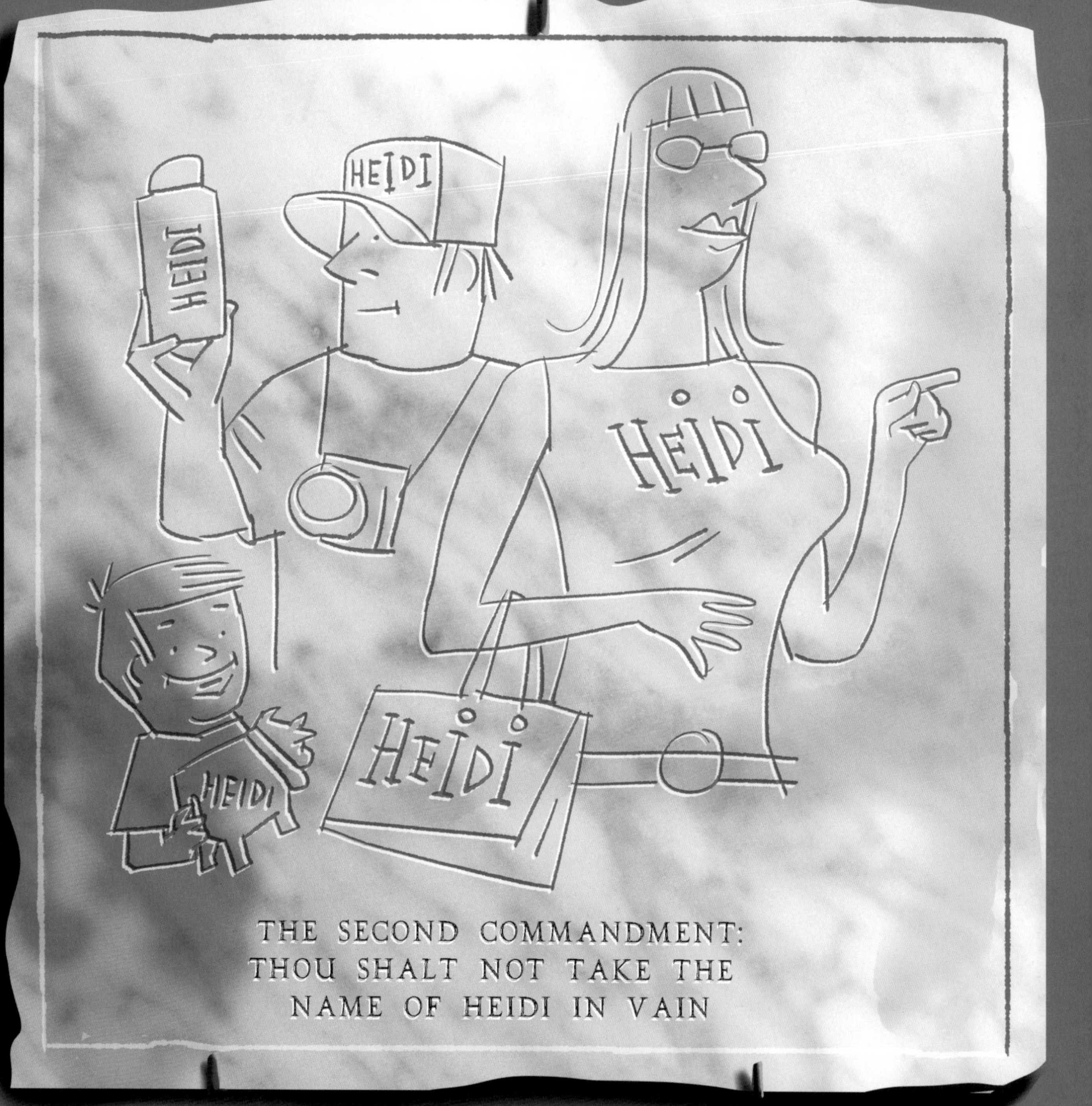
HEIDI
HEIDI
HEIDI
HEIDI
HEIDI
THE SECOND COMMANDMENT:
THOU SHALT NOT TAKE THE
NAME OF HEIDI IN VAIN

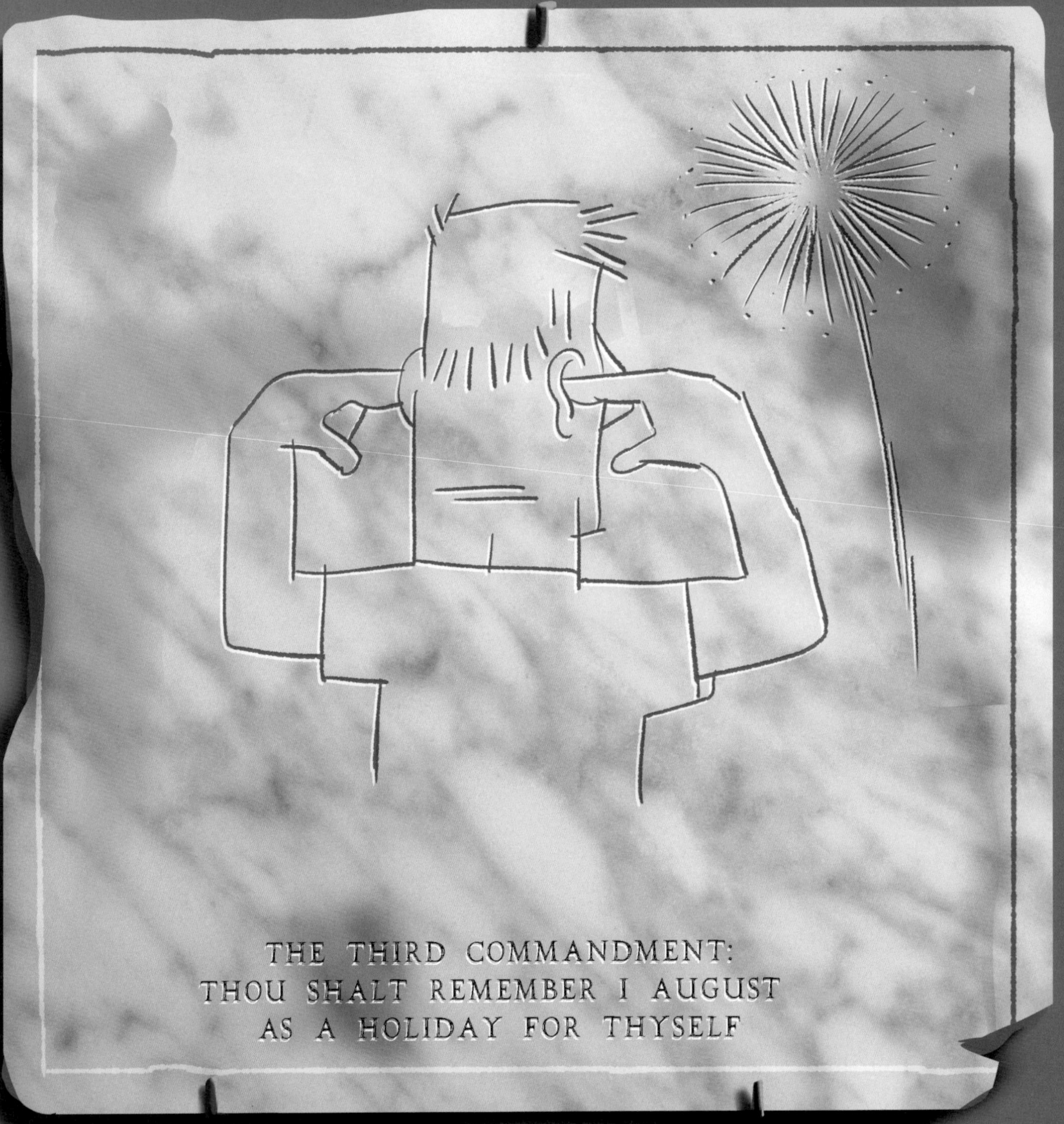
THE THIRD COMMANDMENT:
THOU SHALT REMEMBER I AUGUST
AS A HOLIDAY FOR THYSELF

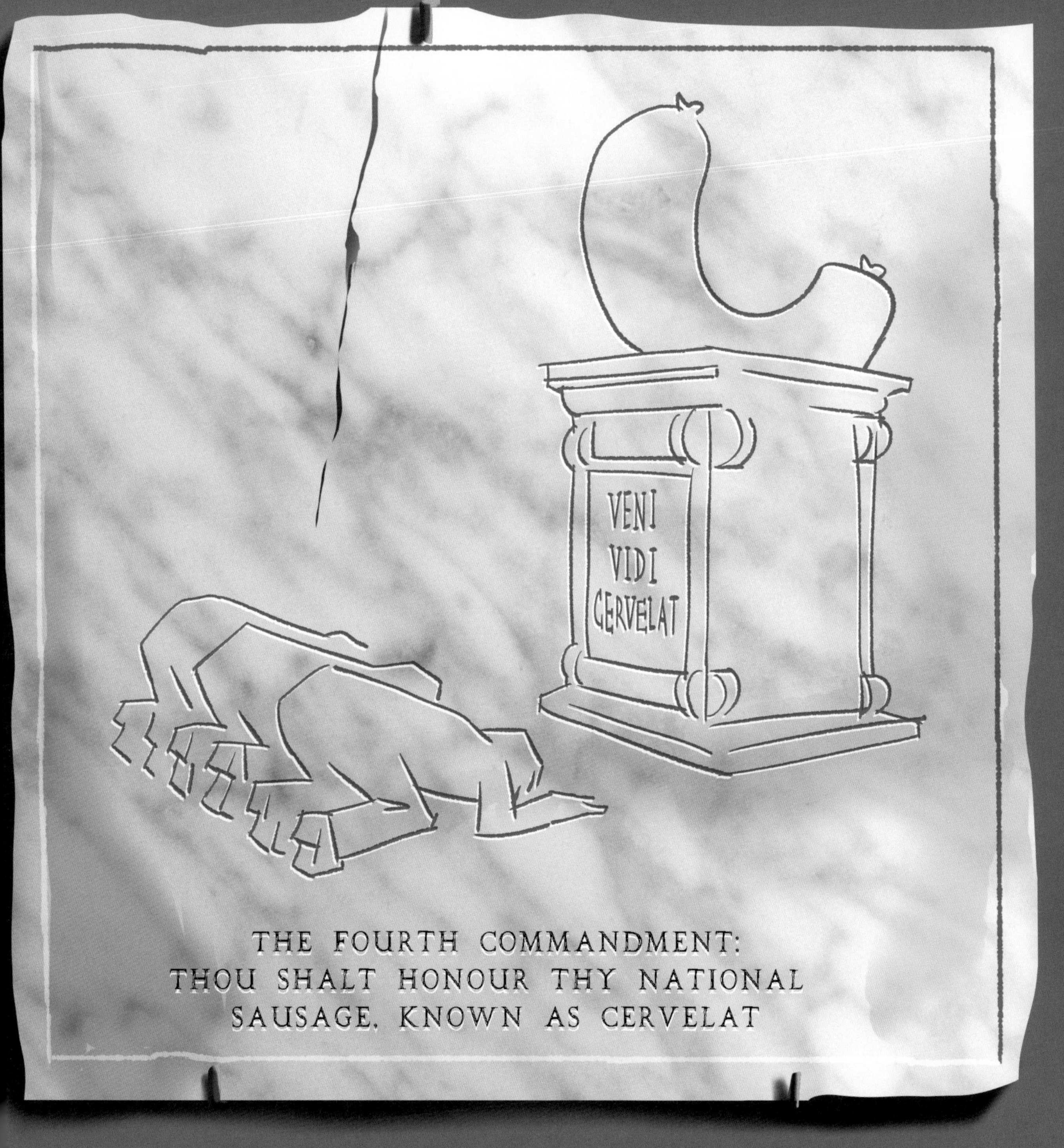
VENI
VIDI
CERVELAT

THE FOURTH COMMANDMENT:
THOU SHALT HONOUR THY NATIONAL
SAUSAGE, KNOWN AS CERVELAT

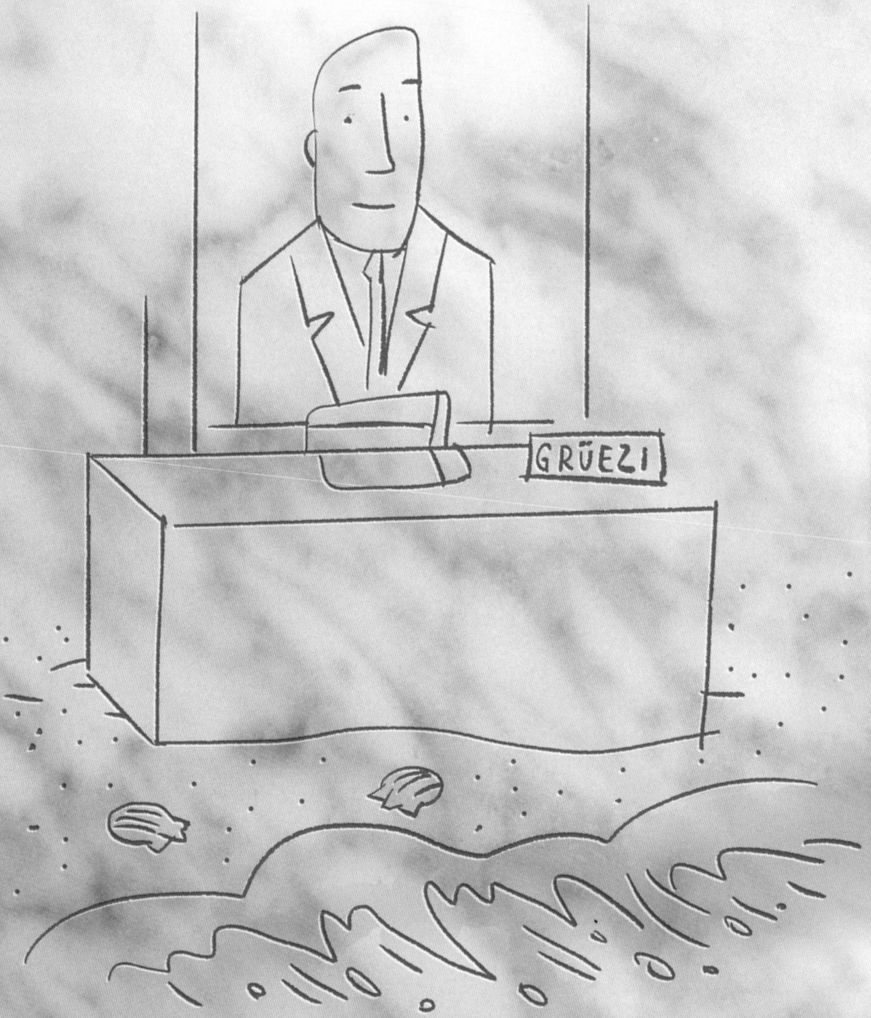
GRÜEZI

THE FIFTH COMMANDMENT:
THOU SHALT SUSTAIN OFFSHORE BANKS
IN THY LANDLOCKED COUNTRY

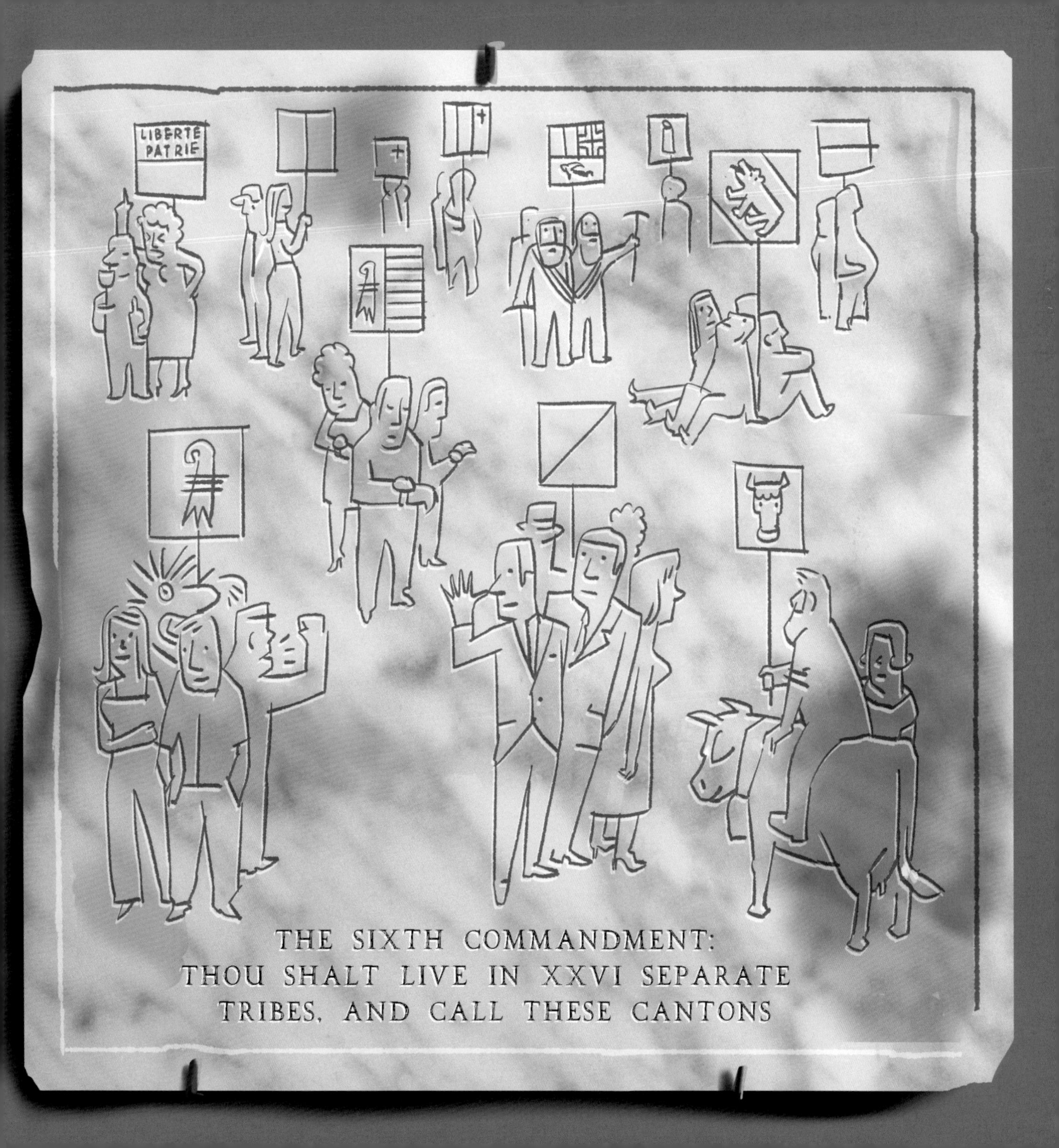
LIBERTÉ
PATRIE

THE SIXTH COMMANDMENT:
THOU SHALT LIVE IN XXVI SEPARATE
TRIBES, AND CALL THESE CANTONS

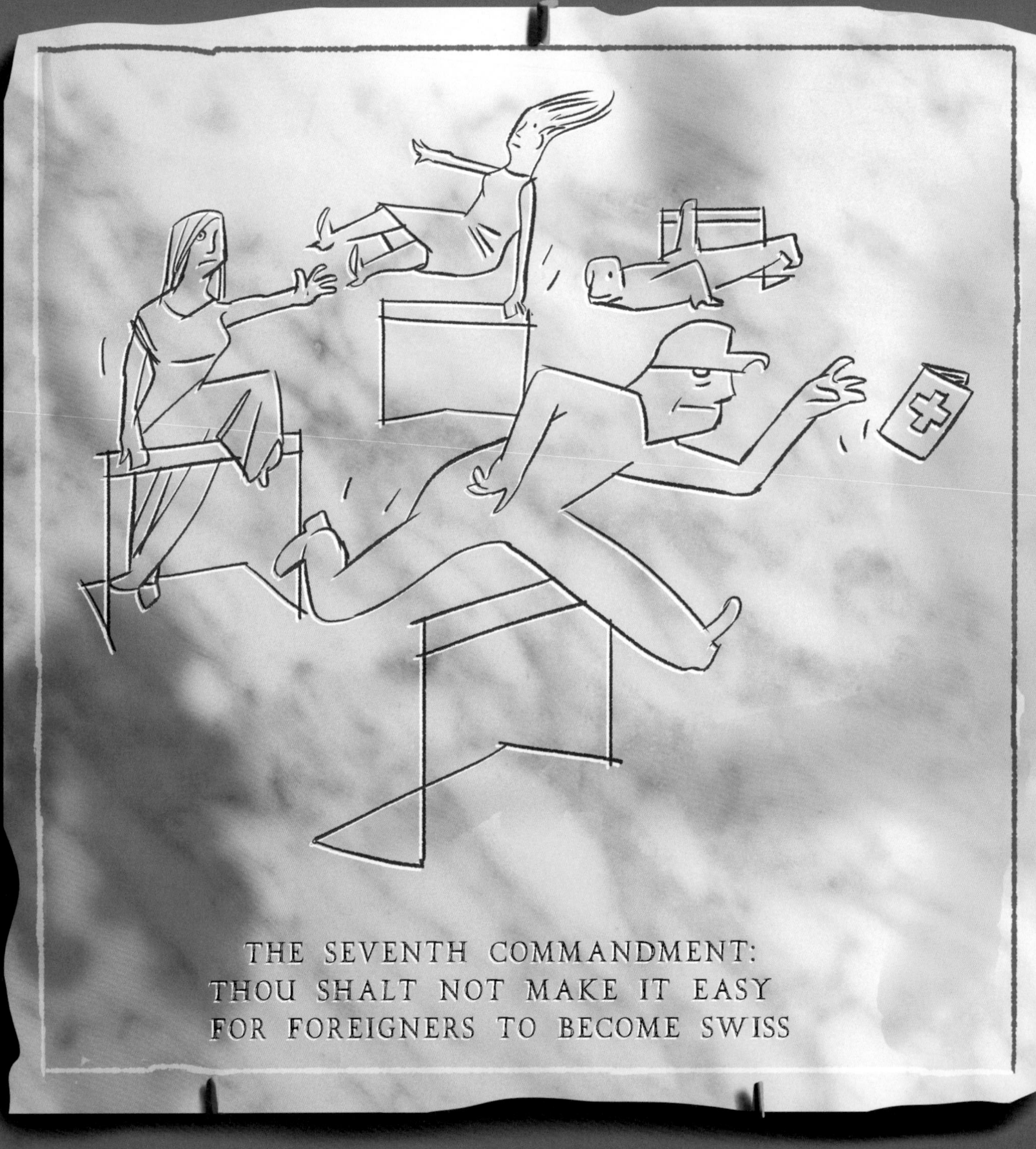
THE SEVENTH COMMANDMENT:
THOU SHALT NOT MAKE IT EASY
FOR FOREIGNERS TO BECOME SWISS

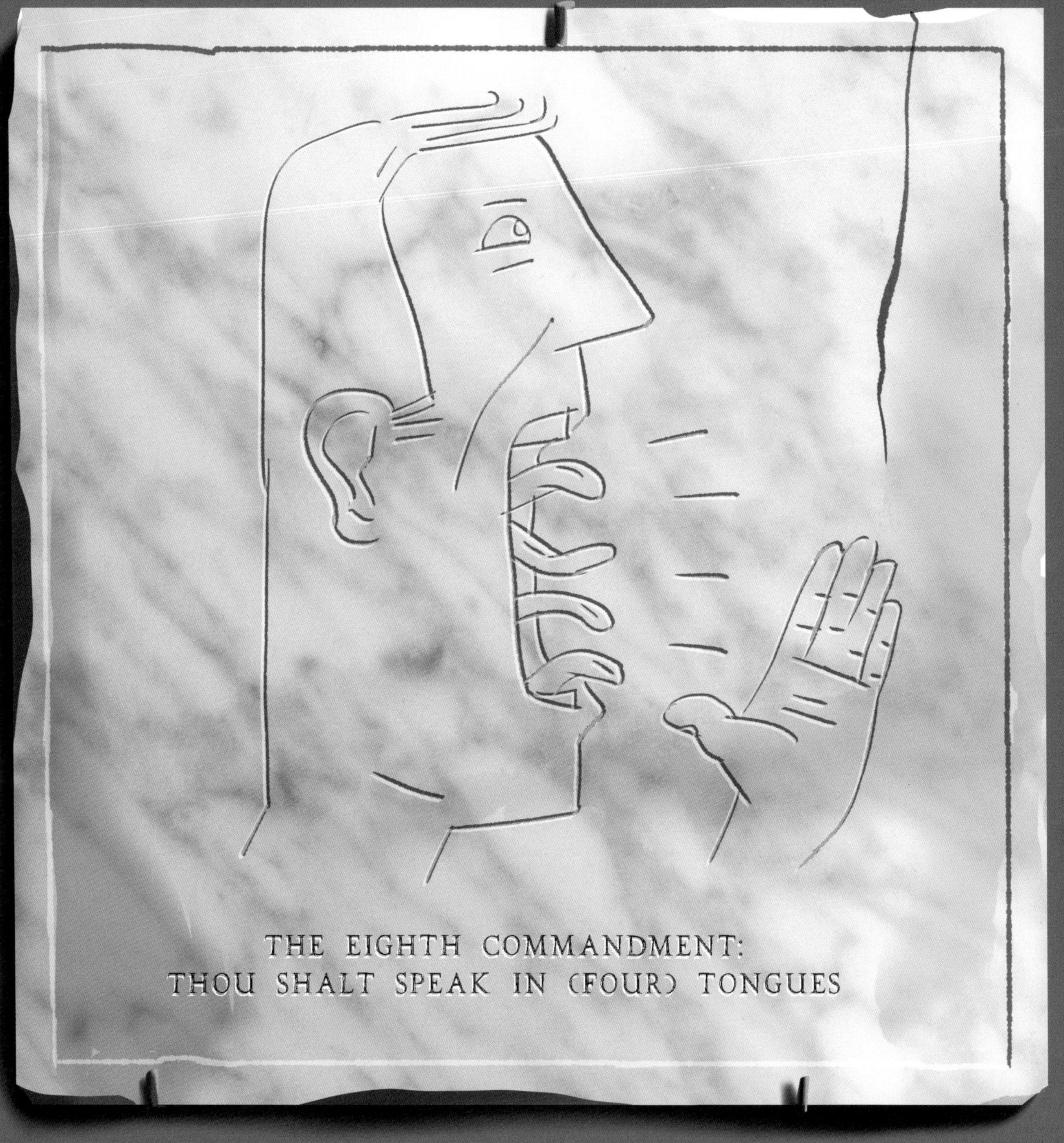
THE EIGHTH COMMANDMENT:
THOU SHALT SPEAK IN (FOUR) TONGUES

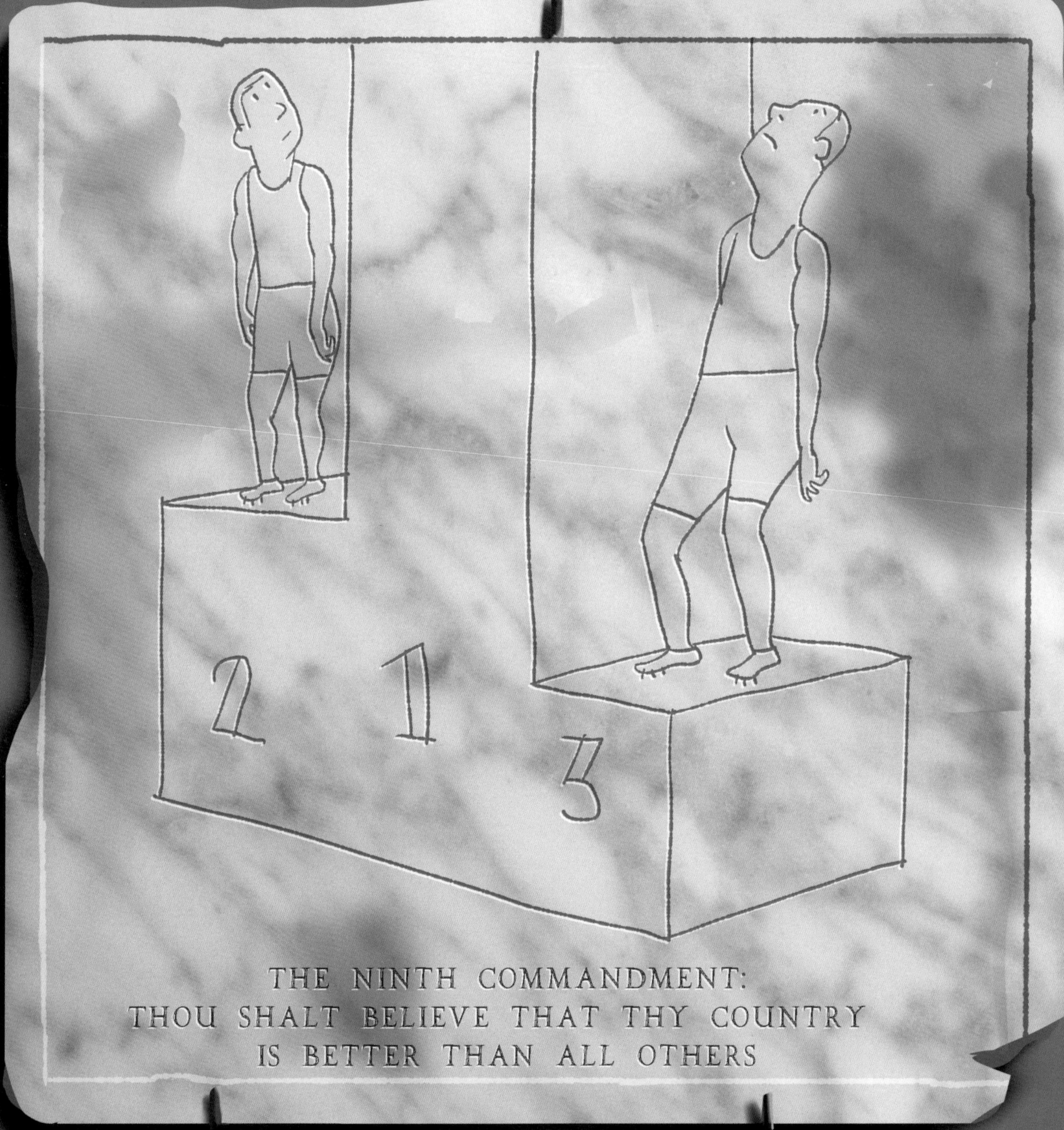
2
1
3
THE NINTH COMMANDMENT:
THOU SHALT BELIEVE THAT THY COUNTRY
IS BETTER THAN ALL OTHERS

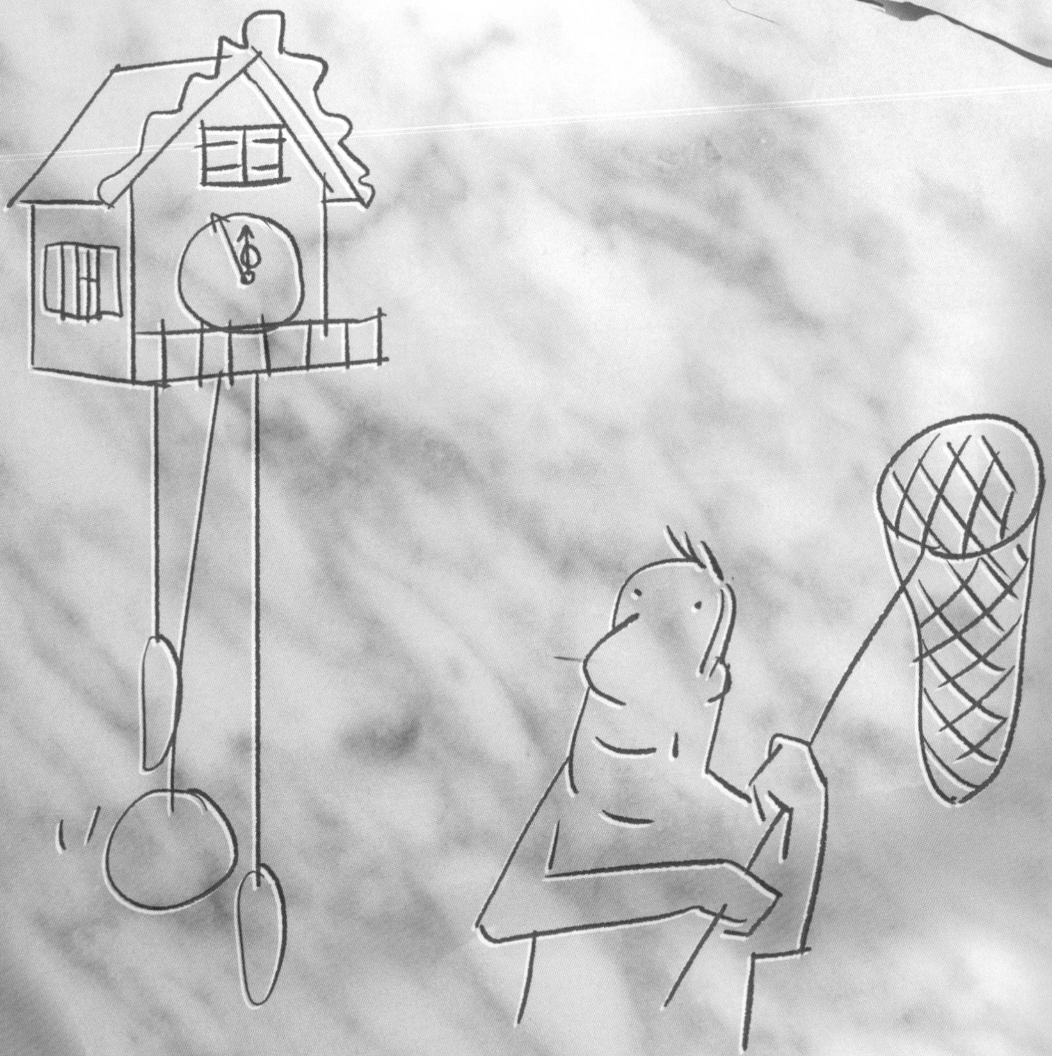

THE TENTH COMMANDMENT:
THOU SHALT COVET THY GERMAN NEIGHBOURS' CUCKOO CLOCKS AND SELL THEM AS YOUR OWN

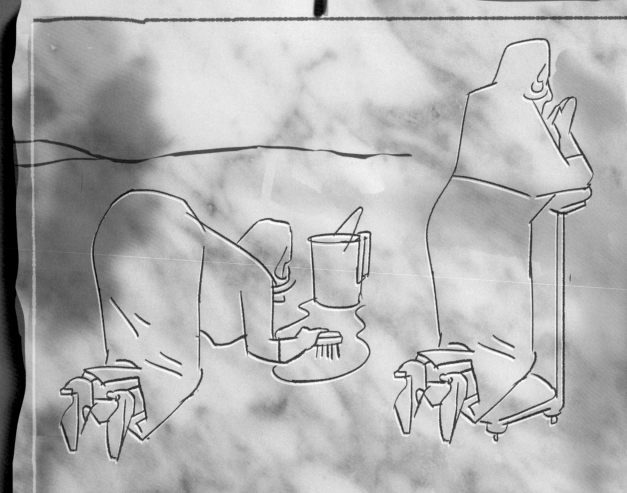

RIGHT   WRONG

THE ELEVENTH COMMANDMENT:
THOU SHALT LIVE THROUGH CLEANLINESS
MORE THAN GODLINESS

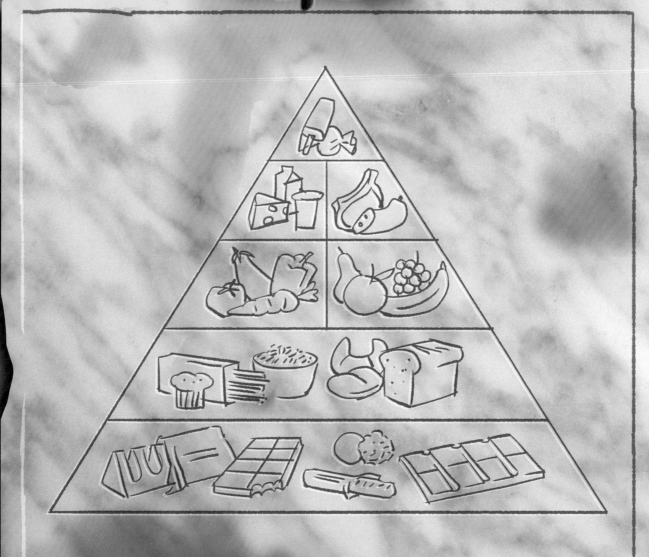

THE TWELFTH COMMANDMENT:
THOU SHALT CONSIDER CHOCOLATE A FOOD
GROUP AND EAT IT EVERY DAY

Step 5:
Finding Swiss happiness
Those moments when you discover the true meaning of Swiss bliss,
whether through swimming, voting or simply saying cheers.

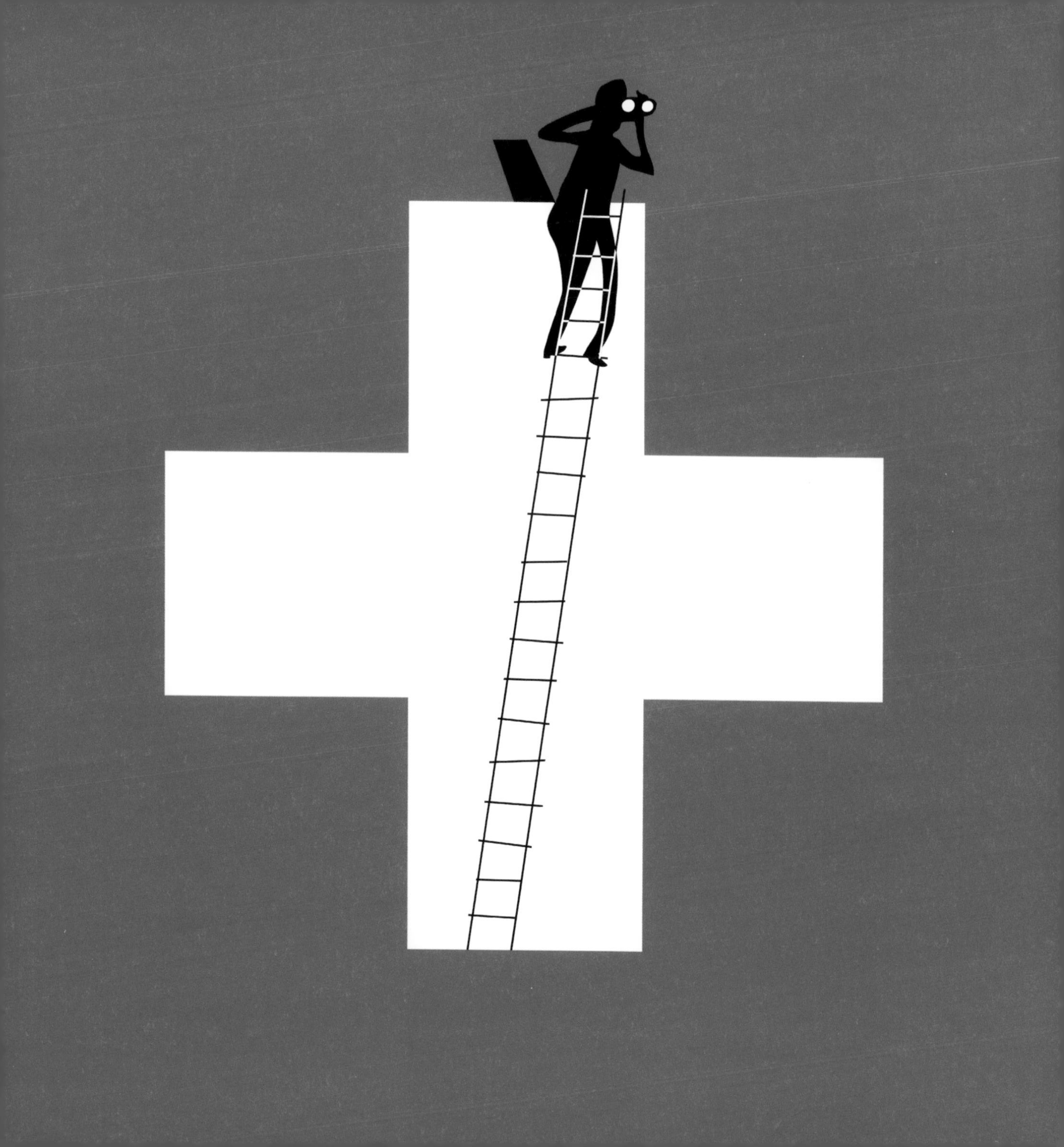

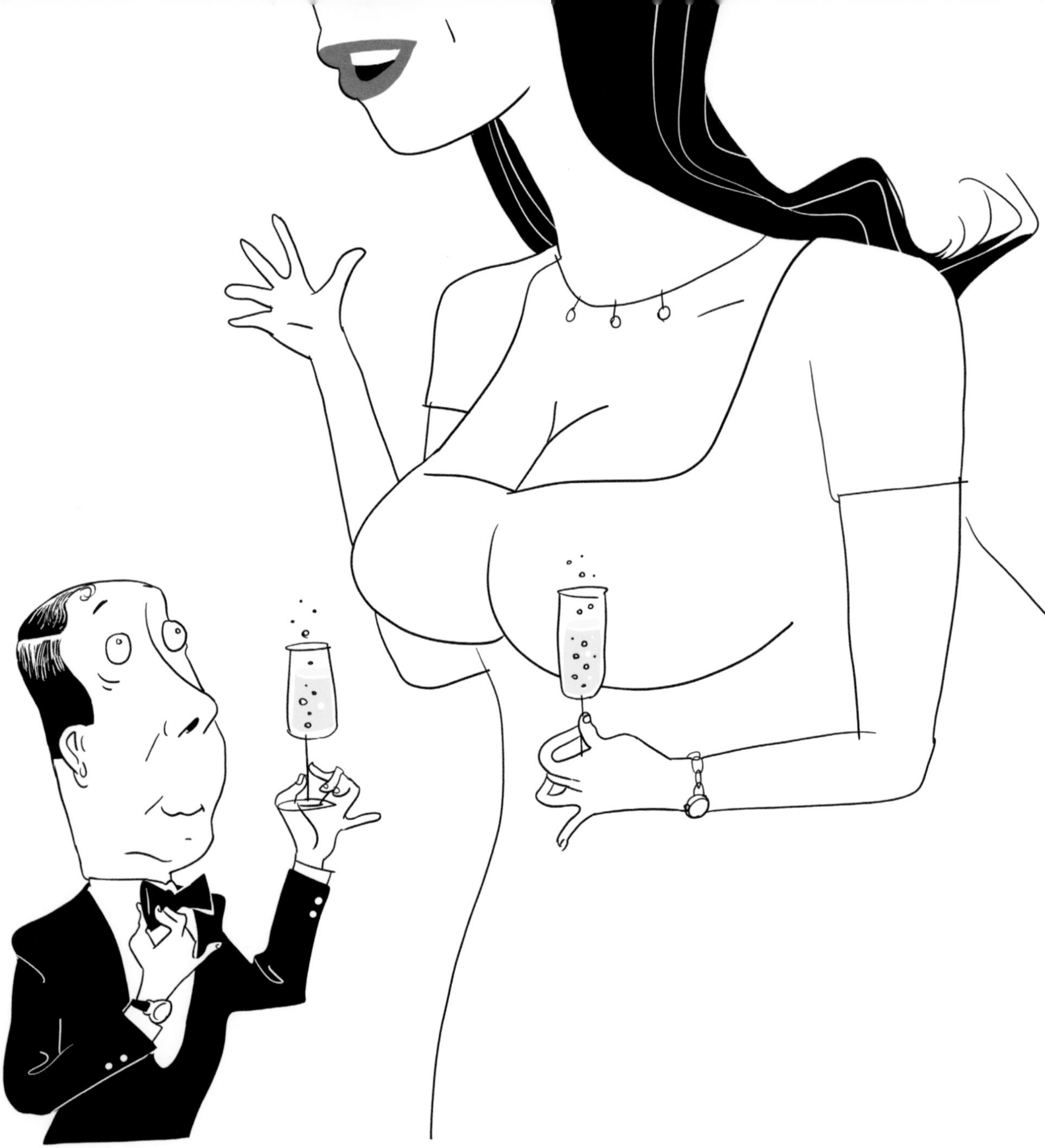

making eye contact when saying cheers with someone

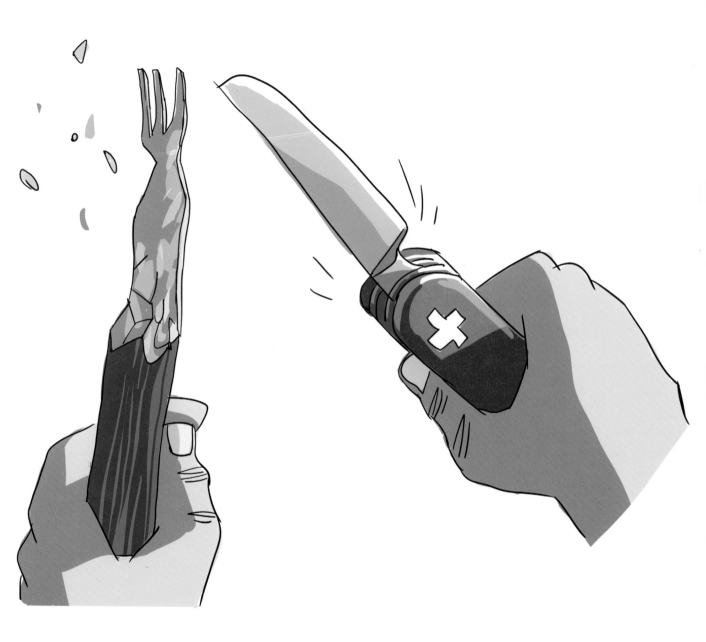

aving a penknife with you to sharpen the stick for cooking the cervelat over the fire

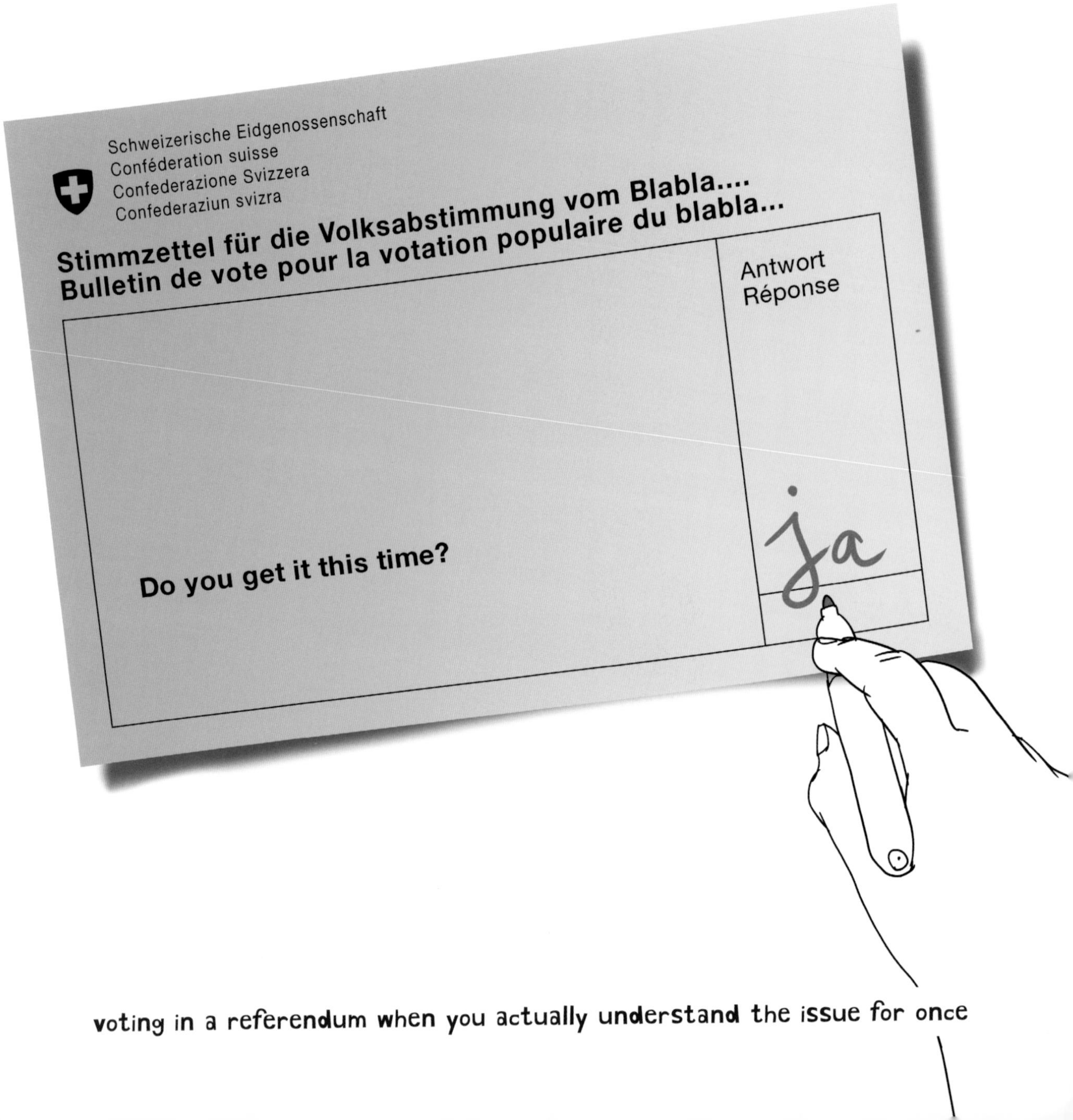
Schweizerische Eidgenossenschaft
Confédération suisse
Confederazione Svizzera
Confederaziun svizra
Stimmzettel für die Volksabstimmung vom Blabla....
Bulletin de vote pour la votation populaire du blabla...
Antwort
Réponse
Do you get it this time?
ja

voting in a referendum when you actually understand the issue for once

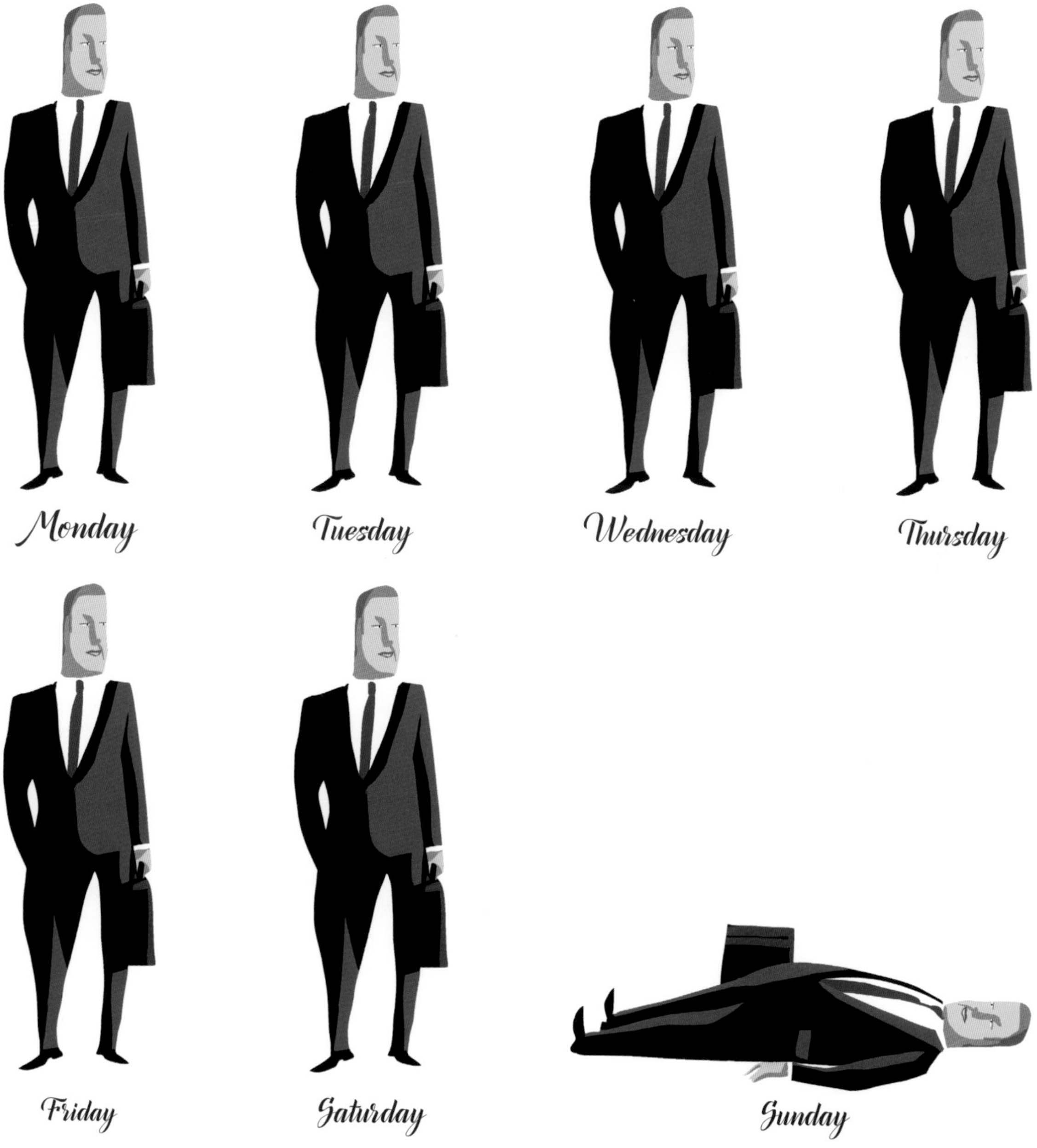
Monday
Tuesday
Wednesday
Thursday
Friday
Saturday
Sunday

enjoying Sunday as a day of relaxation not as one for shopping

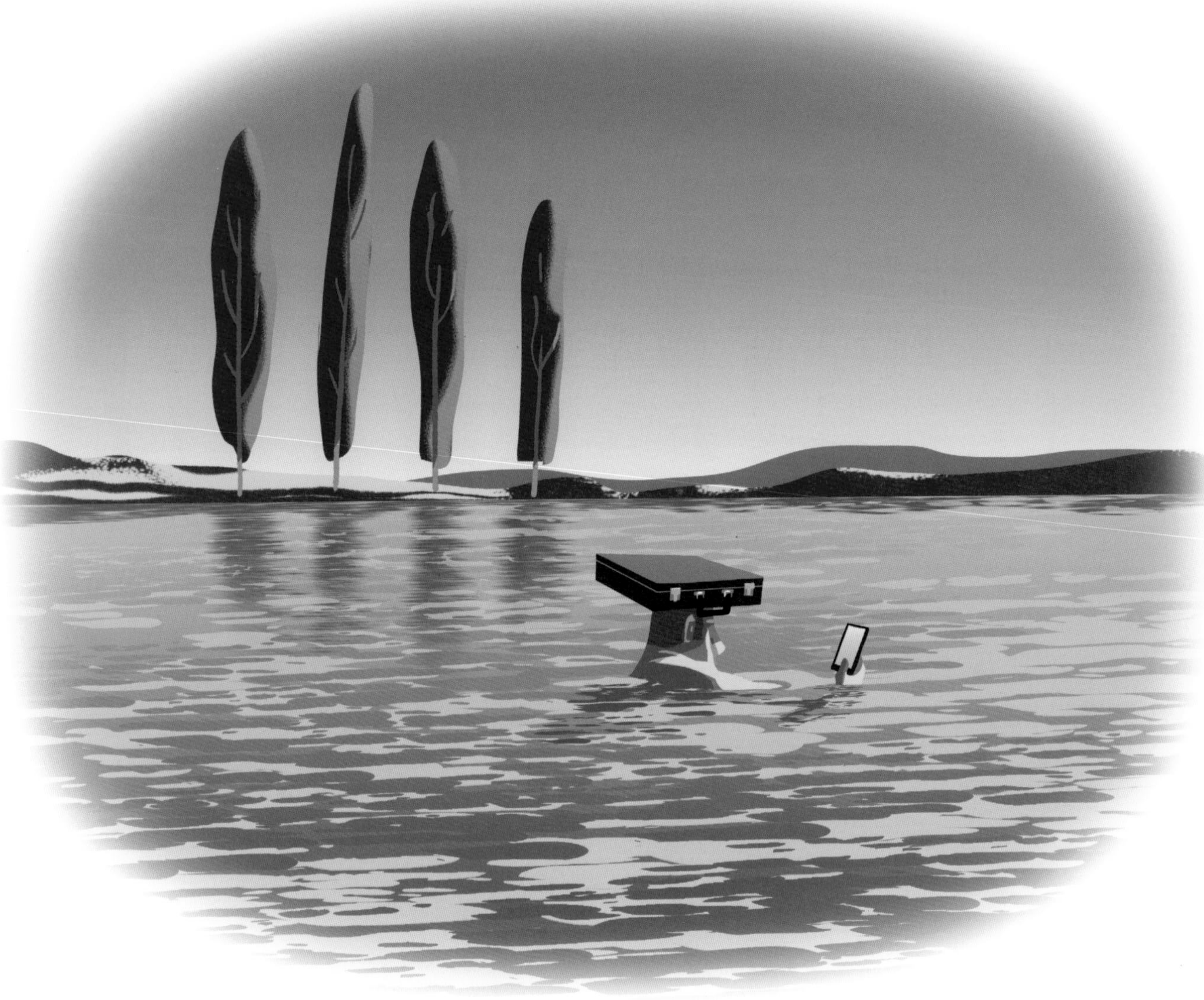

going swimming in the lake or river in your lunch hour

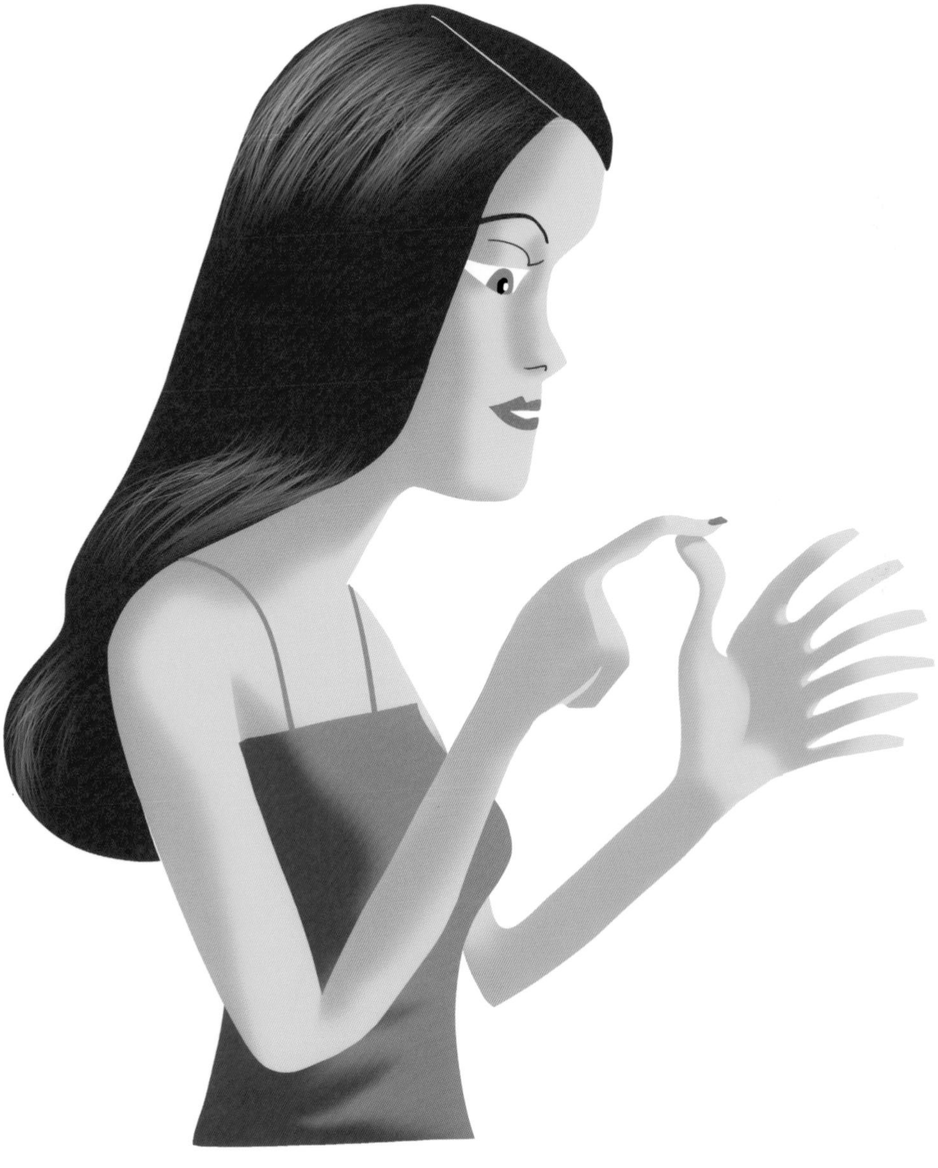

planning your spontaneity a week in advance

Step 6:
A Swiss political crossroads

If you had to decide how to vote on the eight most important topics in Switzerland, this is the political crossroads you would face for each issue.

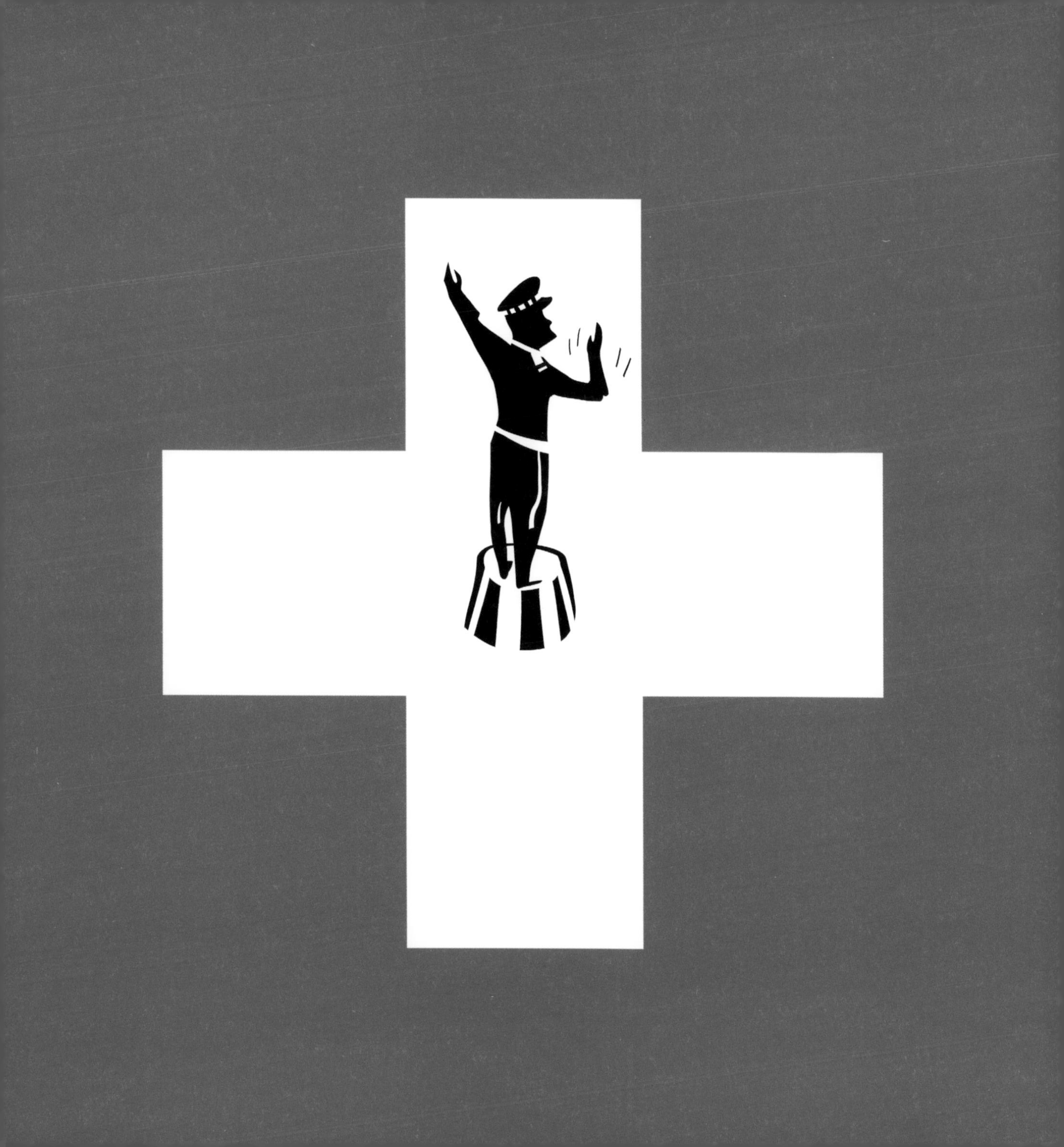

European Union

Switzerland is an island at the centre of the European Union, which accounts for most of its imports and exports. You think:

I just want to go
shopping over the border

Switzerland
should face
reality and
join the
EU tomorrow

the EU is
an evil empire
intent on
destroying
Switzerland

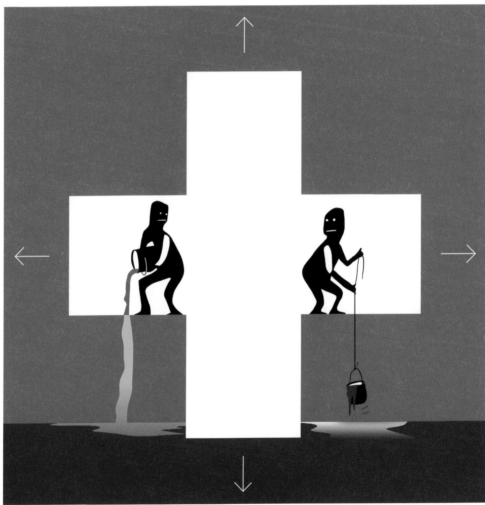

where exactly is the EU?

The army

Switzerland's army is based on a **system of compulsory military service for men.**
You think:

women should also get this paid annual
holiday for doing nothing

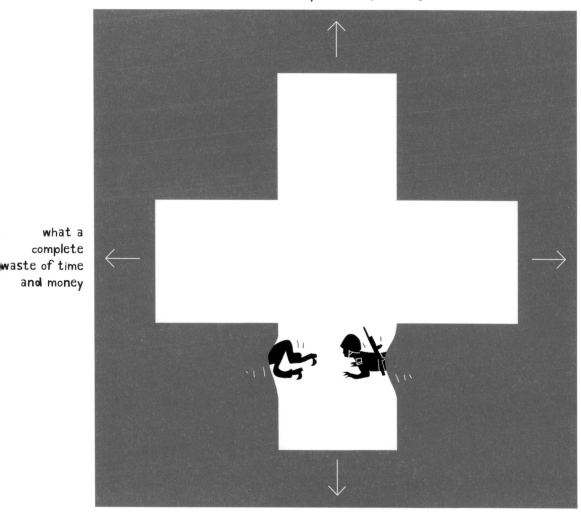

what a
complete
waste of time
and money

the best
army in the
world is
our only
guarantee
of survival

is there a Swiss navy?

Working parents

Gender equality does not cover the Swiss workplace, where **17%** of mothers are in full-time work compared to **85%** of fathers. You think:

I don't care who works as long as someone cooks lunch

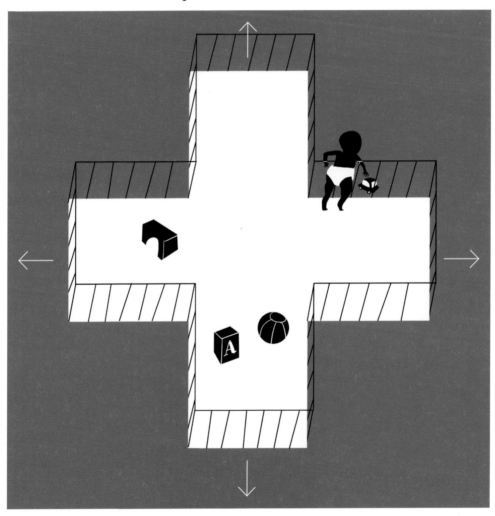

childcare should be free so that everyone can work if they want to

working mothers are emotionally damaging their children

does watching TV count as a full-time job?

Languages

With four national languages, Switzerland is the epitome of a successful multilingual state. You think:

thank God for Google
Translate in meetings

children
should learn
all four so
we can get
along with each
other

everyone
should speak
German
(and I don't
mean High
German)

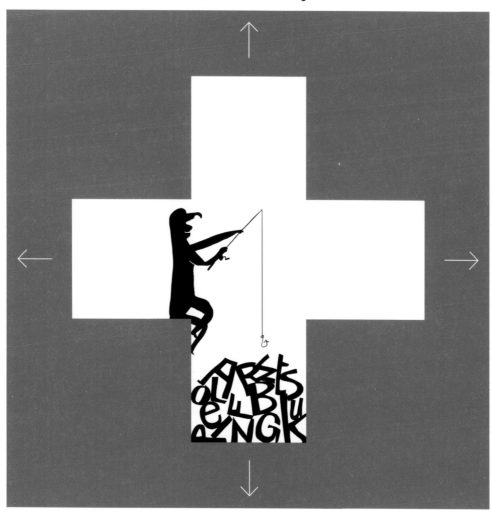

how do you say
"I don't care" in Romansh?

Foreigners

About a quarter of the inhabitants of Switzerland are actually foreigners, ranging from **new arrivals** to those born here. You think:

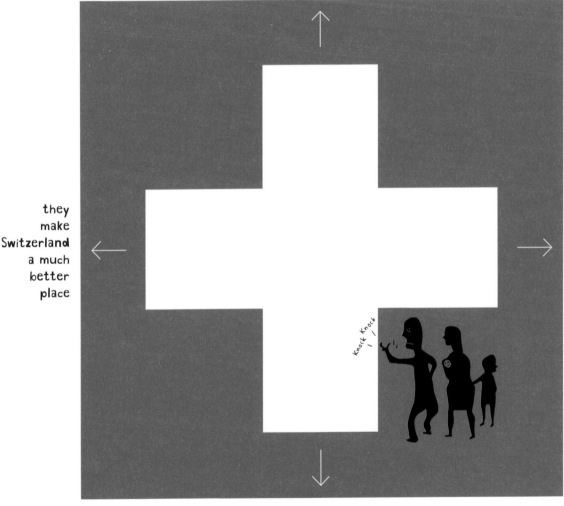

someone has to pick the fruit
and clean the streets

they
make
Switzerland
a much
better
place

deport them
all (except th
millionaires)

if we close the borders
how will I get out?

Knock Knock

Tax

Taxes are set by each community, with wealthy individuals and companies able to negotiate a special rate. You think:

one day I'll be rich enough
to ask for a better tax rate

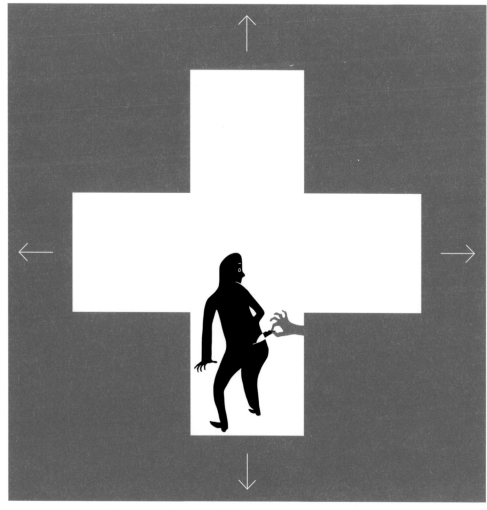

the rich
must be
taxed until
they bleed

taxes
should be
abolished
since all
they do
is fund
benefits

can I choose where my
tax money goes?

Bank secrecy

Banking secrecy in Switzerland is strictly protected by law but this is slowly changing under international pressure. You think:

I wish I could keep my bank account
secret from my wife

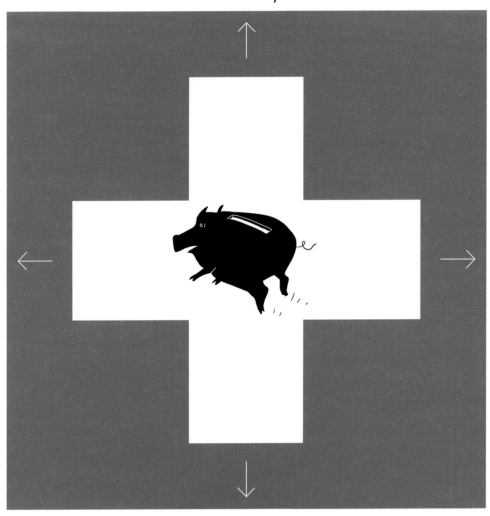

time to
make it
illegal for
non-residents
to have
a Swiss bank
account

there is no
such thing as
dirty money
(as long as
it's in our
vaults)

does keeping your money under the bed
count as a secret bank account?

Direct democracy
Many issues in Swiss politics are decided by a referendum.
You think:

I only vote if something affects
me directly, which is almost never

a great
idea that
has been
hijacked by
racist
populist
rhetoric

fine as
long as
everyone
votes the
way I tell
them to

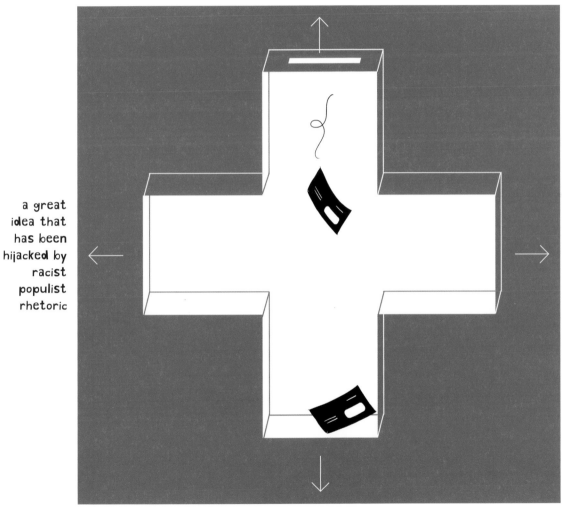

what do you mean I'm supposed
to make these decisions myself?

Step 7:
Laughing with the Swiss
Those moments when you find humour in a land that has a reputation for having none, or in other words, how to put the wit into S-wit-zerland.

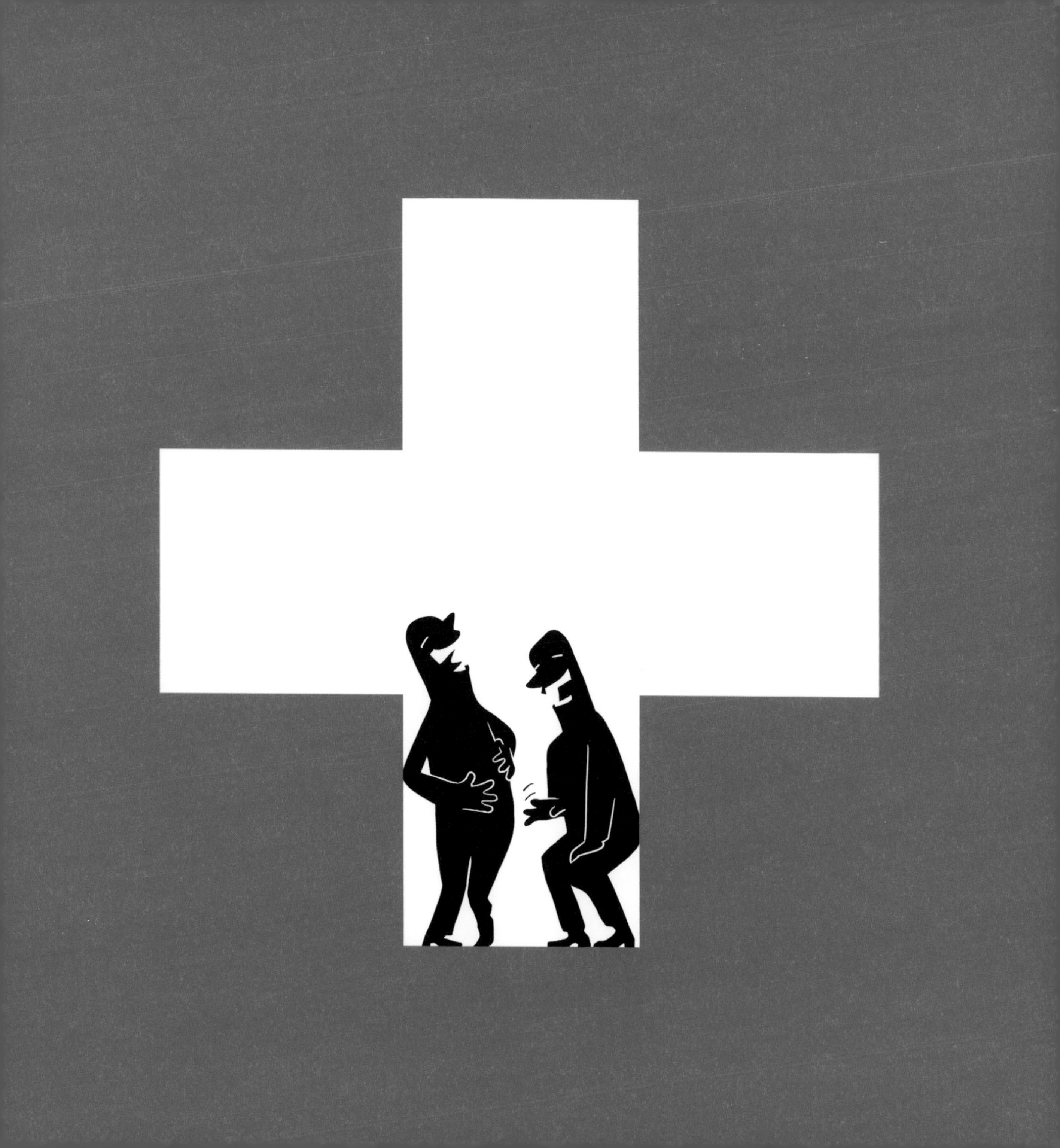

An Austrian family is standing on the Austrian riverbank of the Rhine and want to become Swiss citizens. The border police tell them that all they have to do is swim over to the Swiss side and they'll get the red passport.
The father jumps into the river, swims across while battling the current, clambers out on the other side and proudly receives his Swiss passport.
The mother jumps in next, swallows lots of water, almost goes under but manages to get across. The border police hand her the red booklet.
She shouts at her son to jump into the water and swim as hard as he can.
He does but to no avail: he doesn't make it, and drowns.
The father looks at his tearful wife, shrugs and says:
"Never mind, it was just a bloody foreigner!"

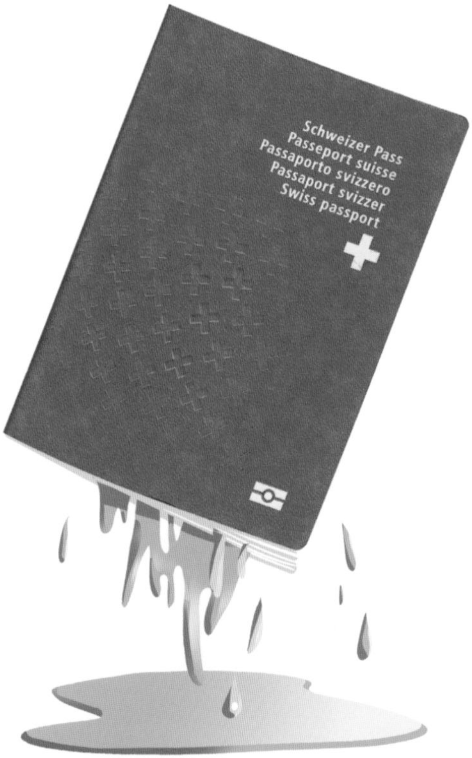
Schweizer Pass
Passeport suisse
Passaporto svizzero
Passaport svizzer
Swiss passport

God created the first Swiss and asked him what he needed.
"Mountains" was the Swiss answer. So God created mountains.
"What do you want next?" asked God. "Cows" said the Swiss.
And God created cows. The Swiss started milking the cow and tasted the milk.
Then he asked God if he also wanted to try it.
God said yes, so the Swiss filled a cup and gave it to him.
Then God asked him: "What do you want now?"
"Five francs sixty rappen."

Five Germans in an Audi Quattro arrive at the border and want to drive into Switzerland. The border guard tells them that's impossible. "Quattro means four," he says "and there are five of you." The Germans answer back, "The vehicle safety certificate states that the car is approved for five people" and insist on speaking to the boss. "Not possible," is the reply "he's arguing with a couple in a Fiat Uno."

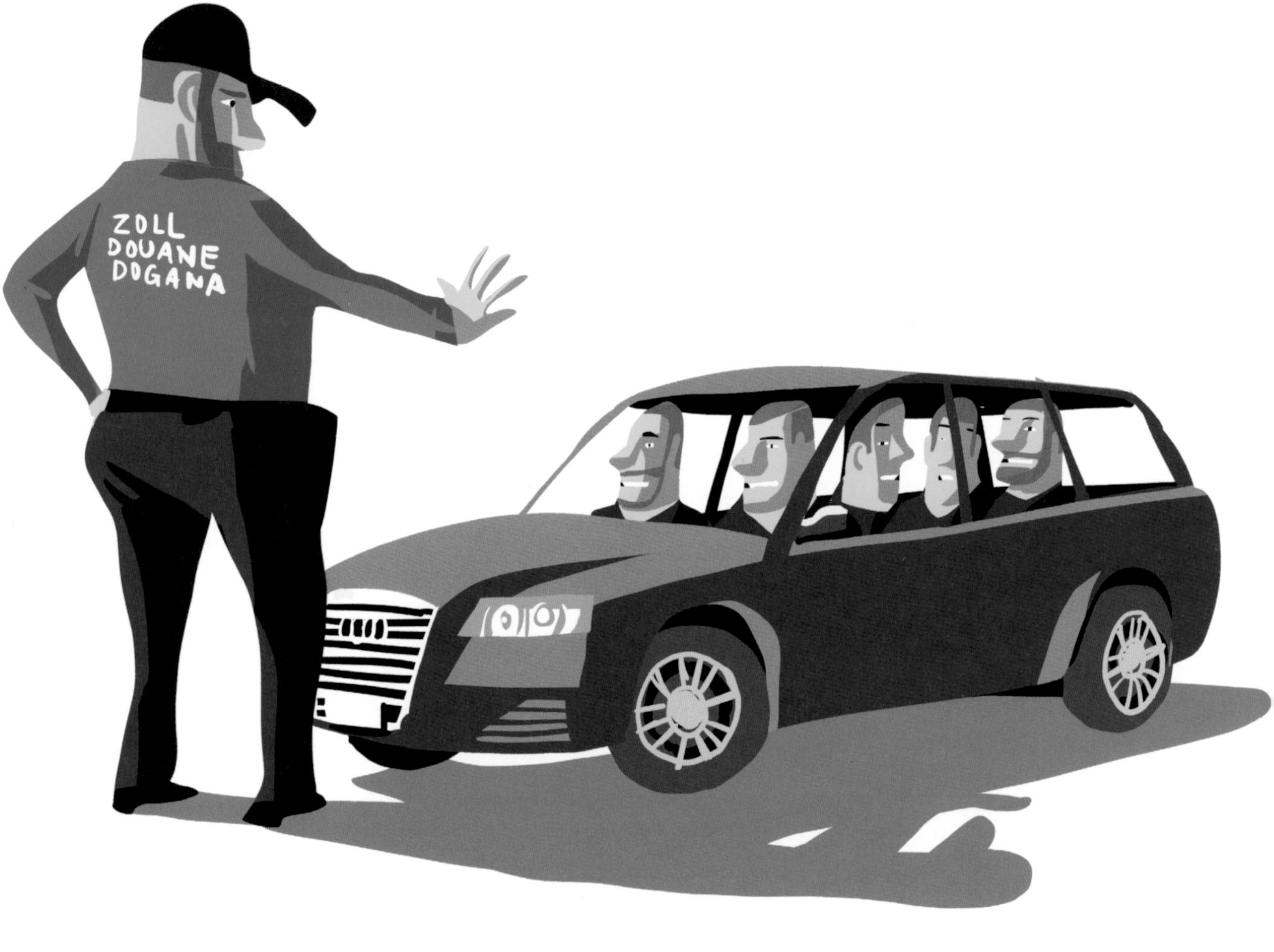
ZOLL
DOUANE
DOGANA

A Russian walks into a Swiss bank with a giant,
heavy suitcase in each of his hands.
He goes to the cashier, brings his face close to the glass and whispers,
"I have two million dollars with me. I urgently need to open a Swiss bank account!"
The Swiss banker replies in a normal volume,
"Sir, there's no need to whisper. Poverty is nothing to be ashamed of in Switzerland."

A Swiss guy, looking for directions, pulls up at a bus stop where
two American tourists are waiting.
"Entschuldigung, sprechen Sie Deutsch?" he asks.
The two Americans just stare at him.
"Excusez-moi, parlez vous Français?" he tries.
The two continue staring.
"Parlare Italiano?" No response. "Discurras ti rumantsch?" Still nothing.
The Swiss guy drives off, extremely annoyed.
The first American turns to the second and says,
"Y'know, maybe we should learn a foreign language."
"Why?" says the other.
"That guy knew four languages and it didn't do him any good."

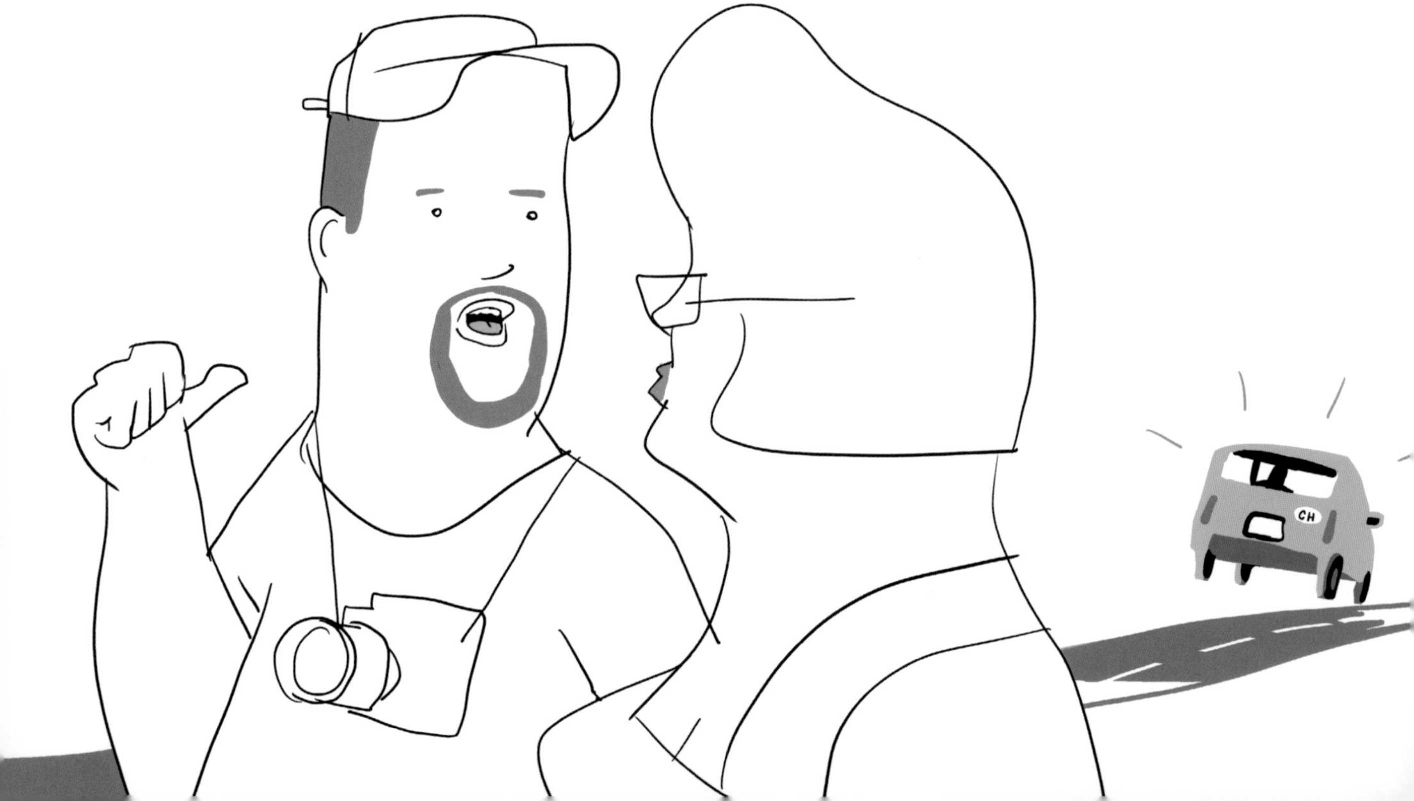
CH

An English girl, a French girl and a Swiss girl are discussing where babies come from.
The English girl says, "In England the stork brings the babies."
The French girl says, "In France Mama and Papa go to bed early
and nine months later there is a new child."
The Swiss girl says, "With us it differs from canton to canton."

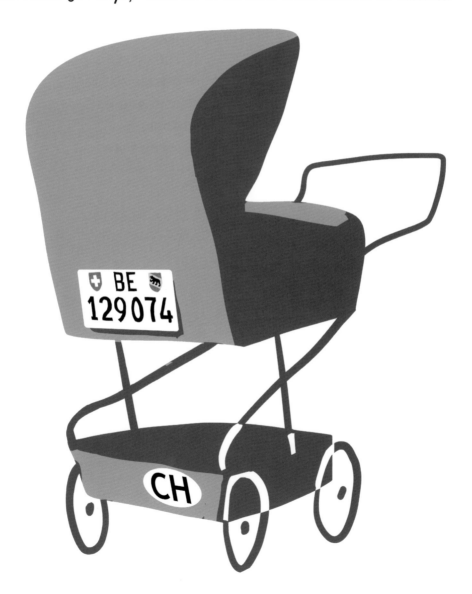

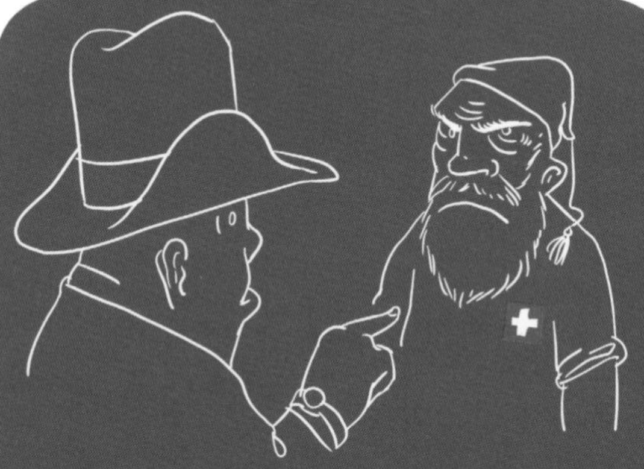

How do you make a Swiss cross?
Ask him if he's from Sweden.

How do you make a Swiss roll?
Push him down
a mountain.

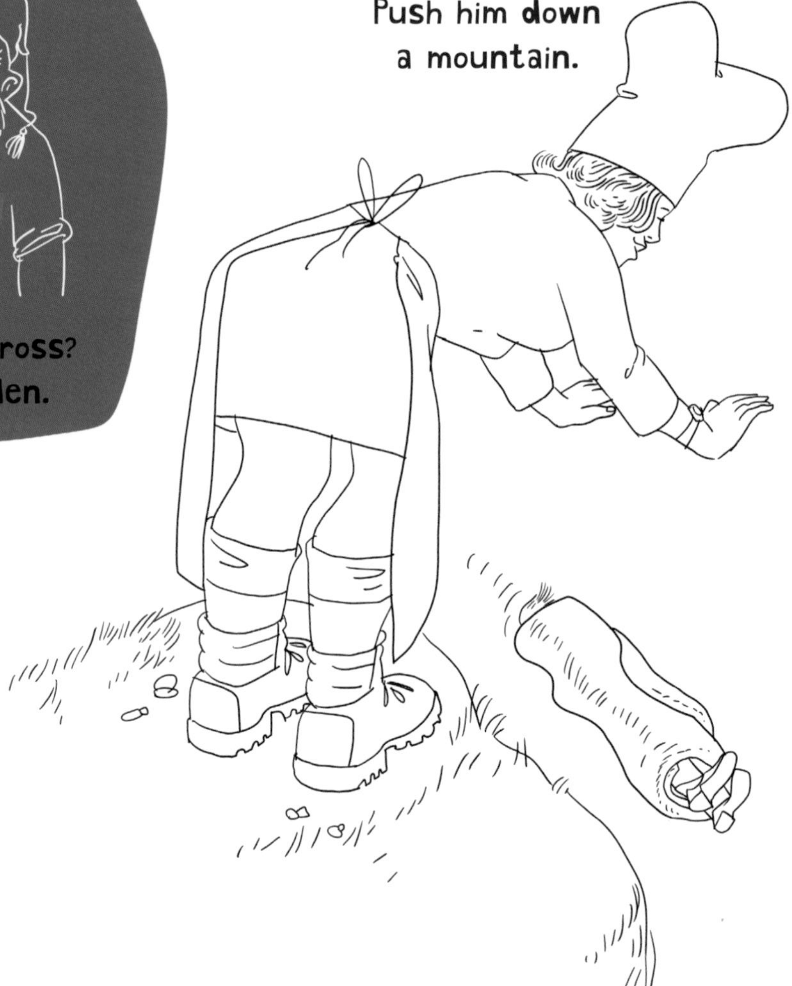

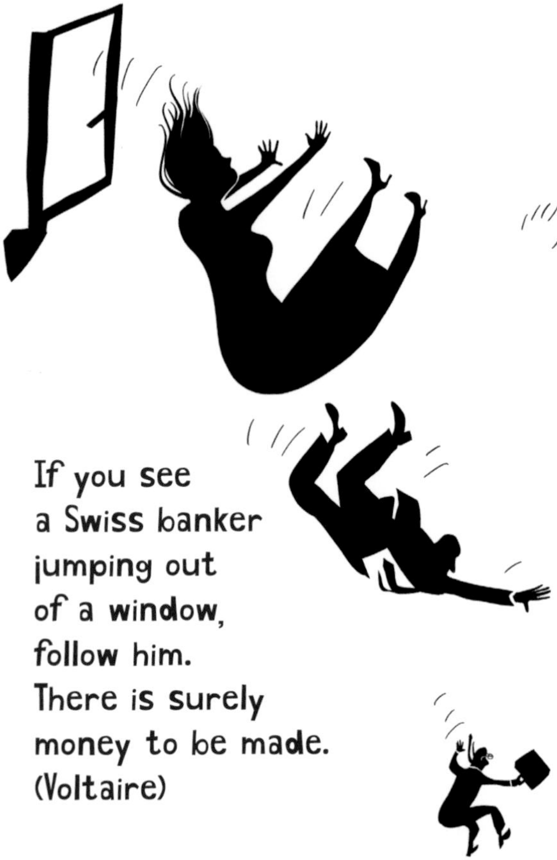

If you see
a Swiss banker
jumping out
of a window,
follow him.
There is surely
money to be made.
(Voltaire)

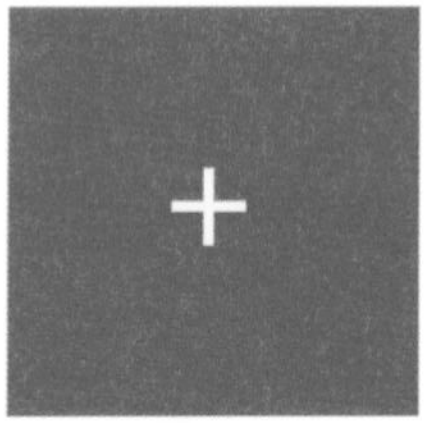

What's the best thing about Switzerland?
Well, the flag is a big plus.

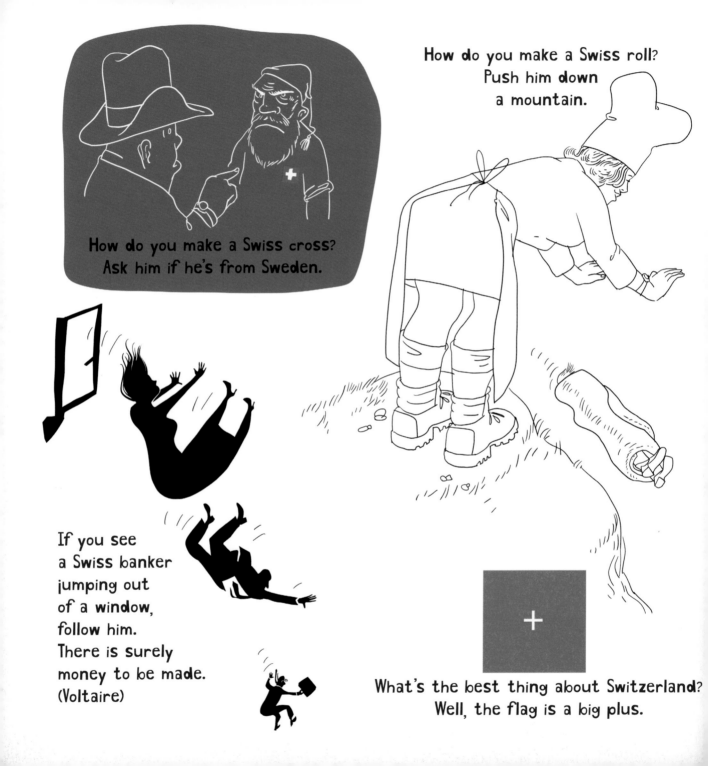

A German, a Serb and a Swiss end up in heaven.
St Peter says to all of them: "Heaven's gate is broken.
Whoever can repair it will be allowed to return to earth. So make me an offer!"
The German replies "I'll do it for 1000 francs".
The Serb says "I'll do it for 200 francs".
The Swiss simply says "2200 francs". St Peter asks him "Why so much?"
And the Swiss replies "1000 for you, 1000 for me and we let the Serb do the work."

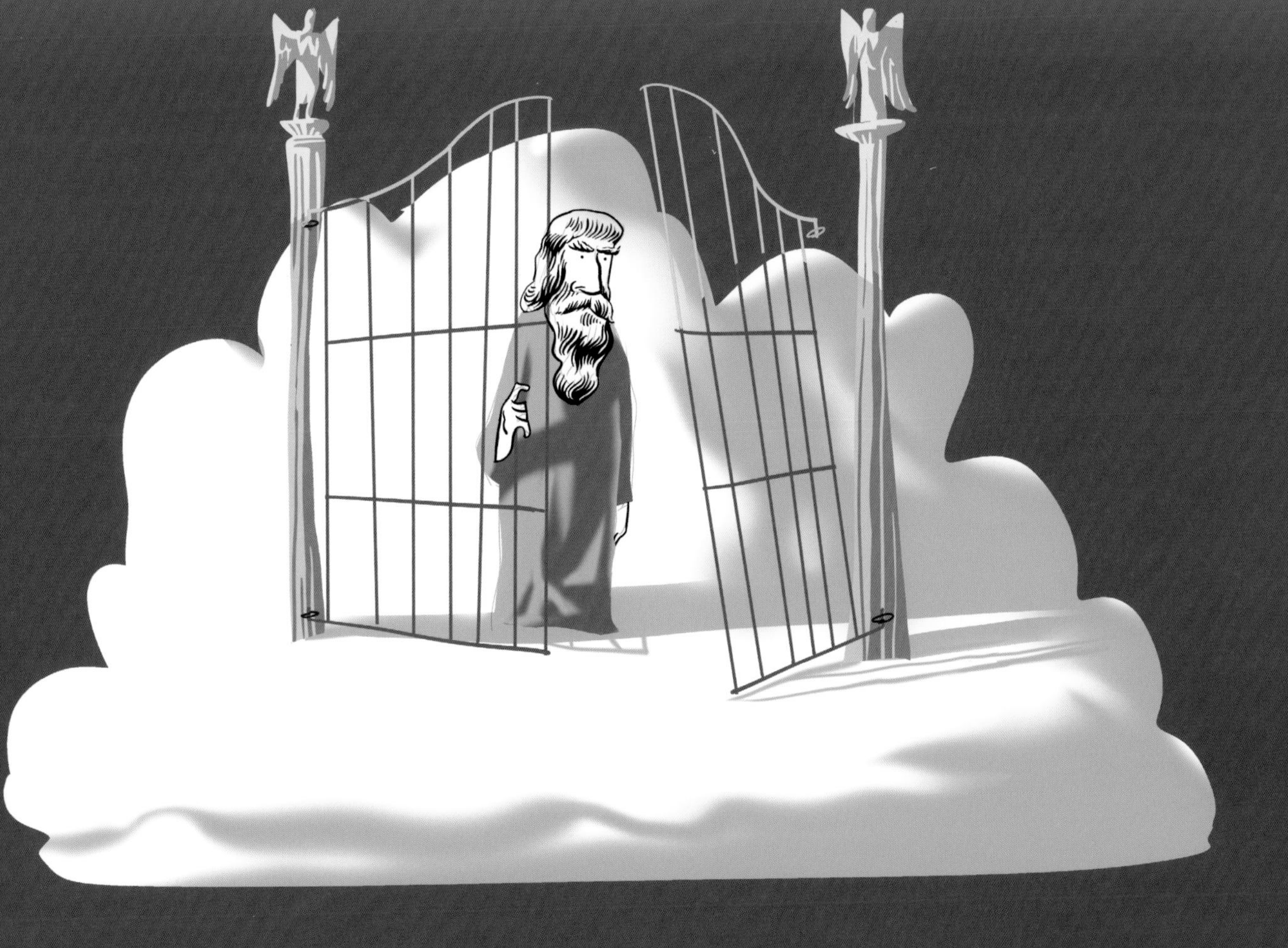

Step 8:
The Swiss view of the world
If the maps of Switzerland, Europe and the world were re-drawn according to a Swiss point of view, this would be the end result.

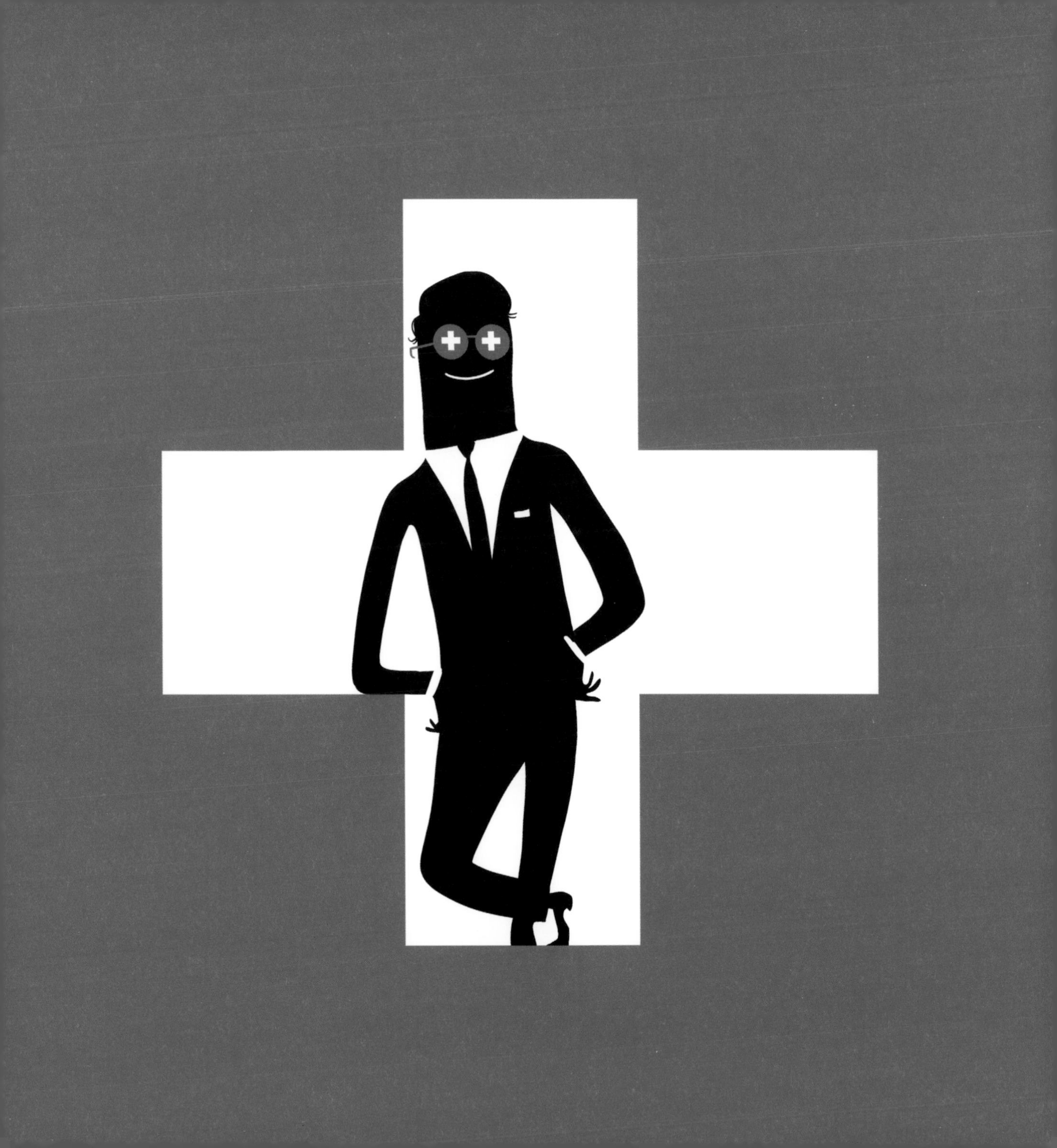

The Treasure Islands

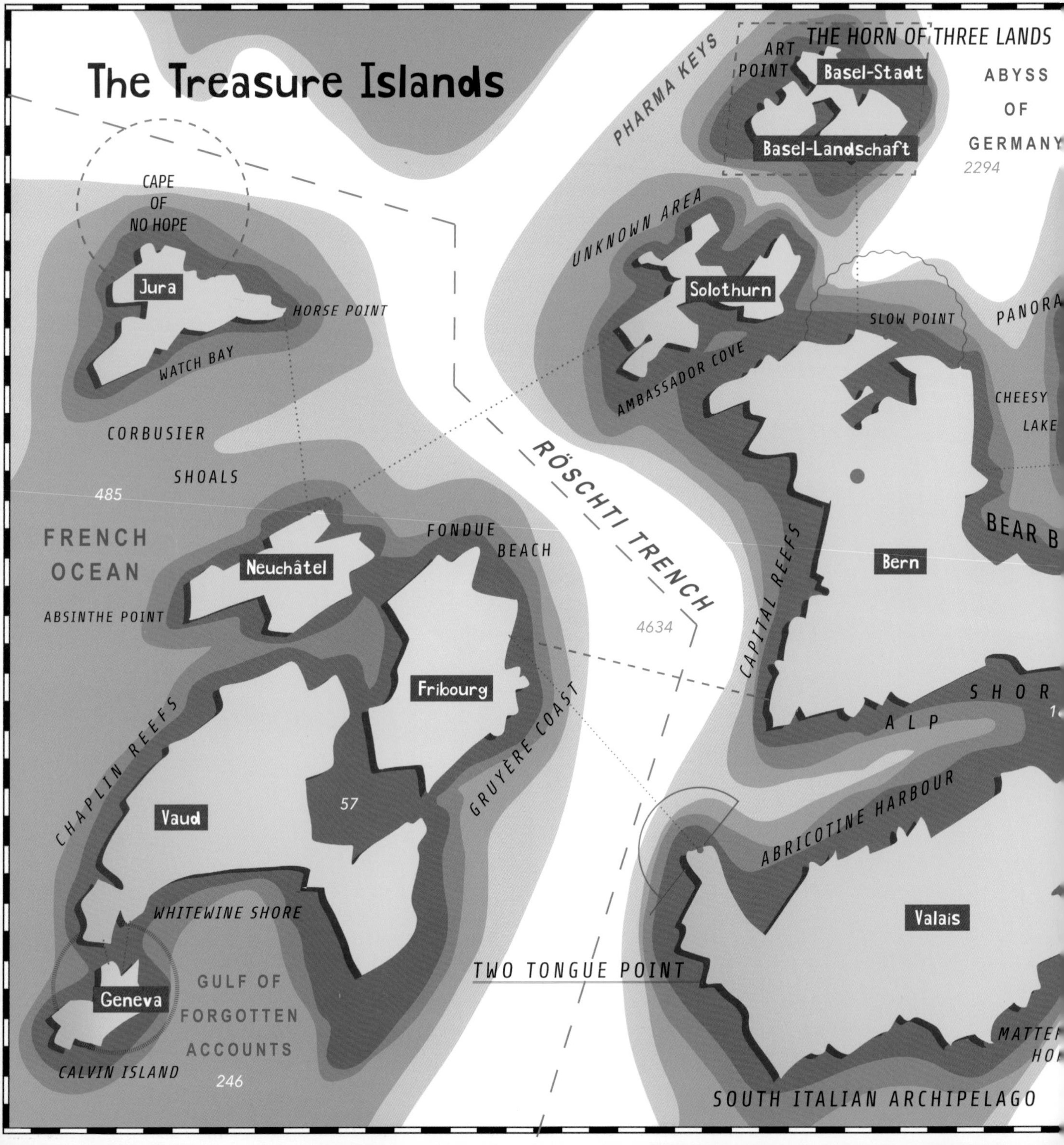
THE HORN OF THREE LANDS
ART POINT
Basel-Stadt
Basel-Landschaft
PHARMA KEYS
ABYSS OF GERMANY
2294
CAPE OF NO HOPE
Jura
HORSE POINT
WATCH BAY
UNKNOWN AREA
Solothurn
SLOW POINT
PANORA
AMBASSADOR COVE
CHEESY LAKE
CORBUSIER SHOALS
485
RÖSCHTI TRENCH
BEAR B
FRENCH OCEAN
FONDUE BEACH
Neuchâtel
Bern
CAPITAL REEFS
ABSINTHE POINT
4634
Fribourg
SHOR
ALP
CHAPLIN REEFS
GRUYÈRE COAST
Vaud
57
ABRICOTINE HARBOUR
Valais
WHITEWINE SHORE
TWO TONGUE POINT
GULF OF FORGOTTEN ACCOUNTS
Geneva
CALVIN ISLAND
246
MATTE
SOUTH ITALIAN ARCHIPELAGO

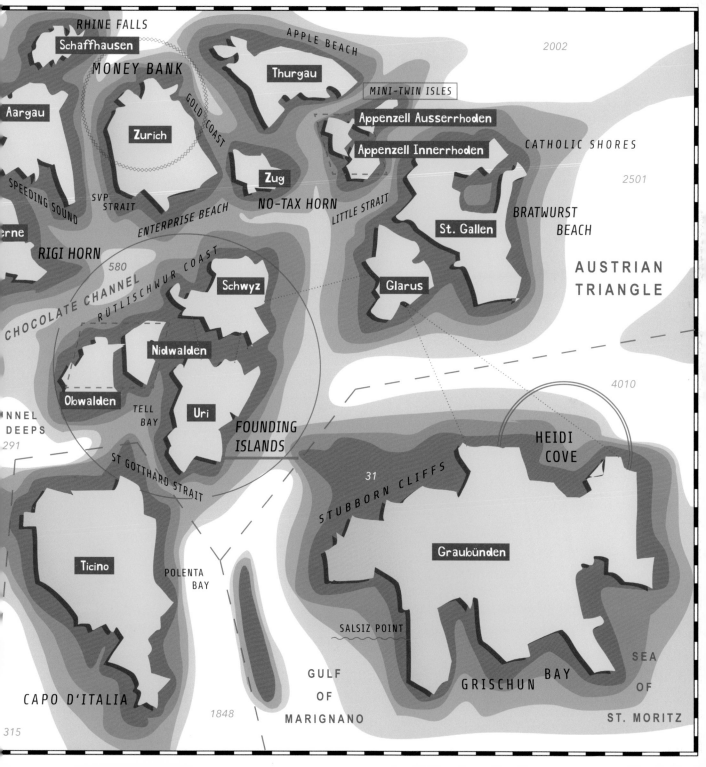

RHINE FALLS

Schaffhausen

MONEY BANK

APPLE BEACH

2002

Thurgau

MINI-TWIN ISLES

Aargau

GOLD COAST

Appenzell Ausserrhoden

Appenzell Innerrhoden

CATHOLIC SHORES

Zurich

2501

Zug

SPEEDING SOUND

SVP STRAIT

NO-TAX HORN

LITTLE STRAIT

St. Gallen

BRATWURST BEACH

ENTERPRISE BEACH

rne

RIGI HORN

CHOCOLATE CHANNEL

580

RÜTLISCHWUR COAST

Schwyz

Glarus

AUSTRIAN TRIANGLE

NNEL DEEPS

291

Nidwalden

Obwalden

TELL BAY

Uri

FOUNDING ISLANDS

4010

HEIDI COVE

ST GOTTHARD STRAIT

31

STUBBORN CLIFFS

Graubünden

Ticino

POLENTA BAY

SALSIZ POINT

SEA

OF

CAPO D'ITALIA

1848

GULF

OF

MARIGNANO

GRISCHUN BAY

ST. MORITZ

315

The Swiss view of Europe

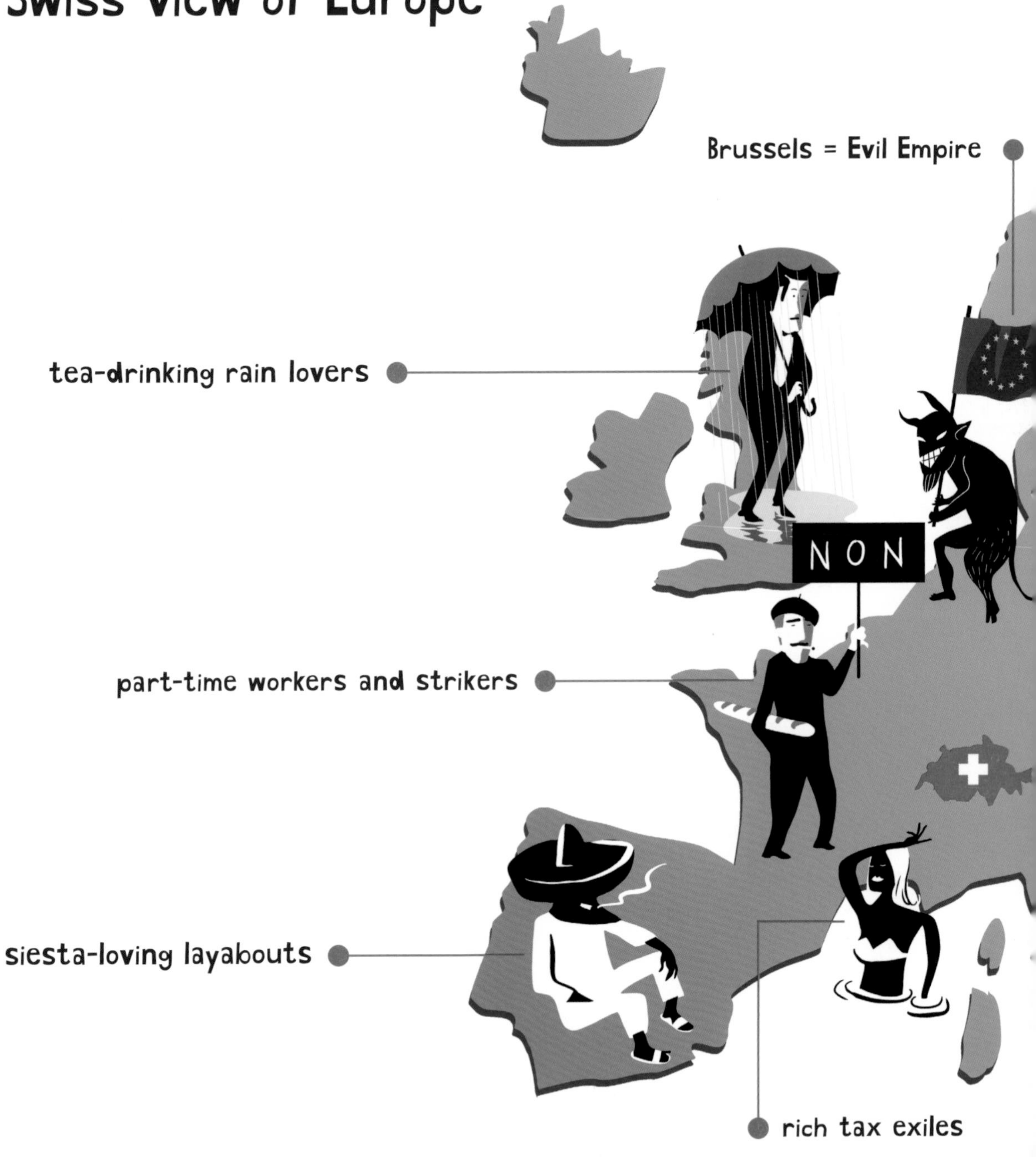

Brussels = Evil Empire
tea-drinking rain lovers
NON
part-time workers and strikers
siesta-loving layabouts
rich tax exiles

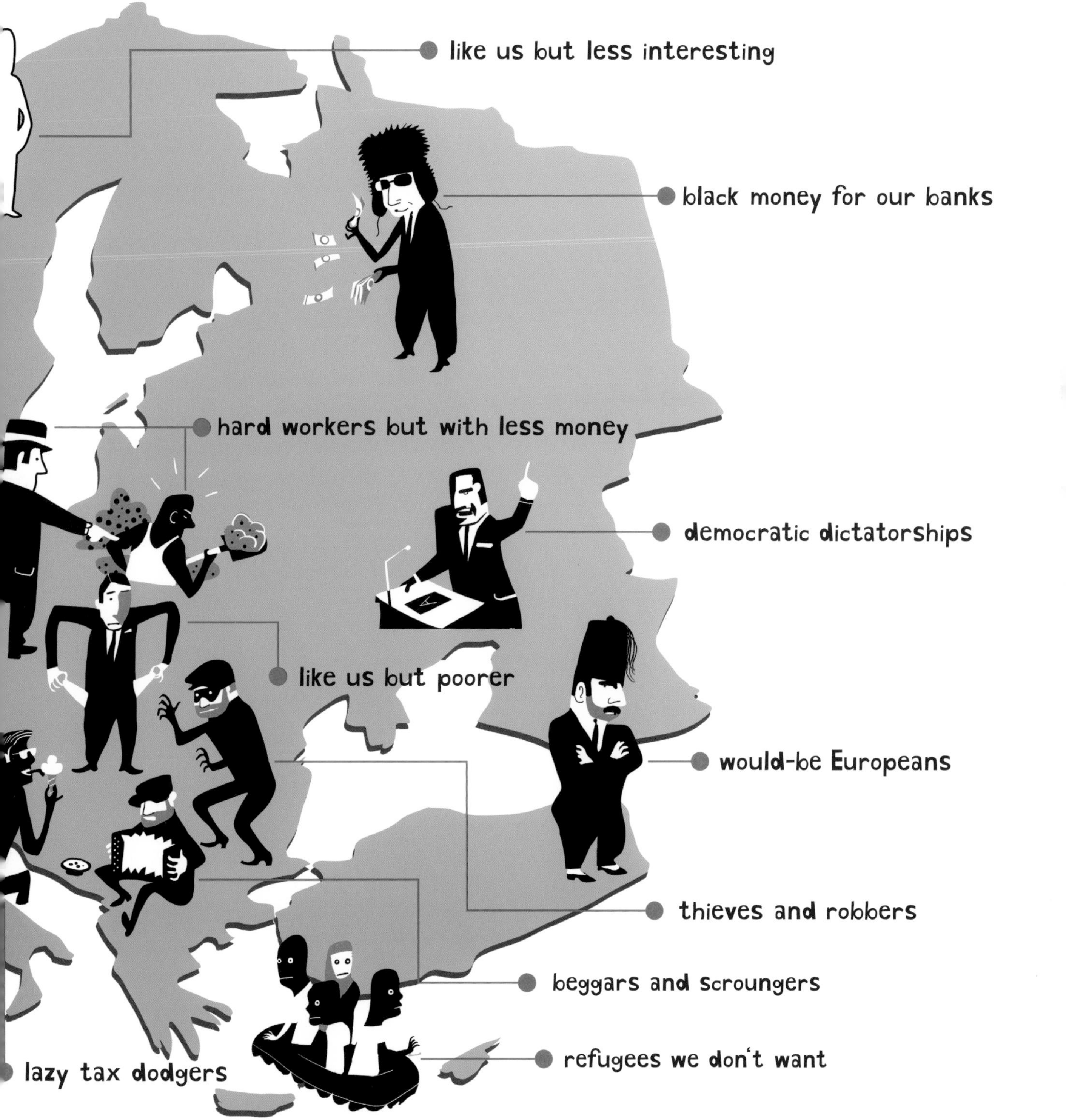
like us but less interesting
black money for our banks
hard workers but with less money
democratic dictatorships
like us but poorer
would-be Europeans
thieves and robbers
beggars and scroungers
lazy tax dodgers
refugees we don't want

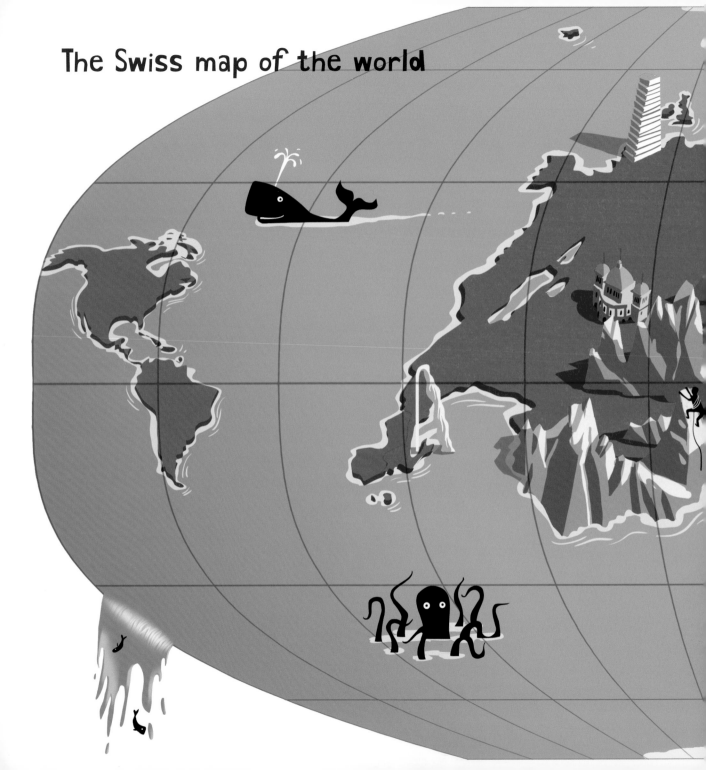

The Swiss map of the world

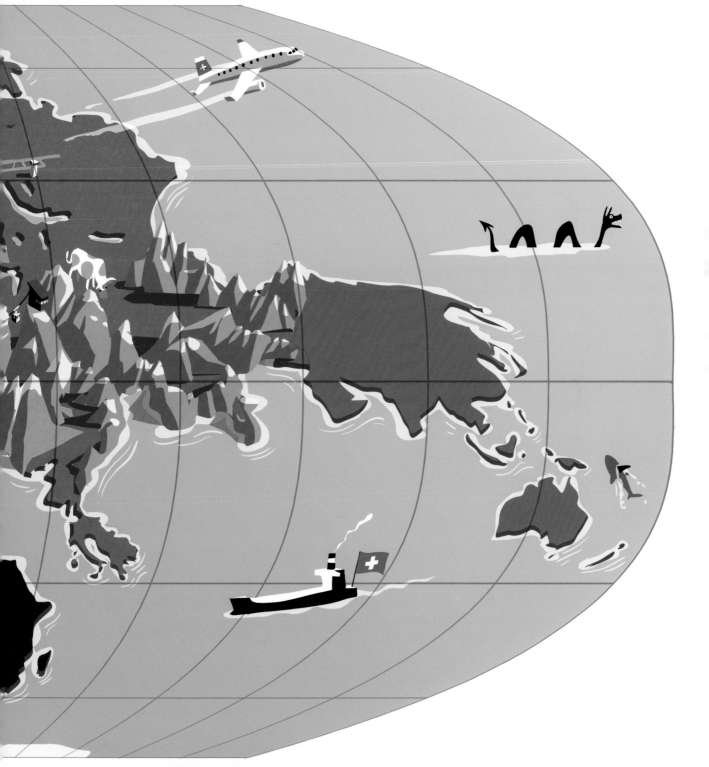

Conclusion

Well done! You've reached the end of your Swissness discovery programme. If you've made it this far without any major social disasters or international incidents, then you have mastered the art of How to be Swiss. In fact, whether you've lived here all your life or just a short while, you can probably now call Switzerland home.

By the same authors: The hilarious cartoon book of German-English false friends

A chef using a preservative is not quite the same as a Chef using a Präservativ. False friends like these are a foreign language's booby traps: words that are similar to ones we know but which have very different meanings. Whether you are learning English or German, or consider yourself an expert in both, this book will make you laugh—and maybe also learn something too.

Diccon Bewes and Michael Meister

CHF 14.90

ISBN 978-3-905252-85-9

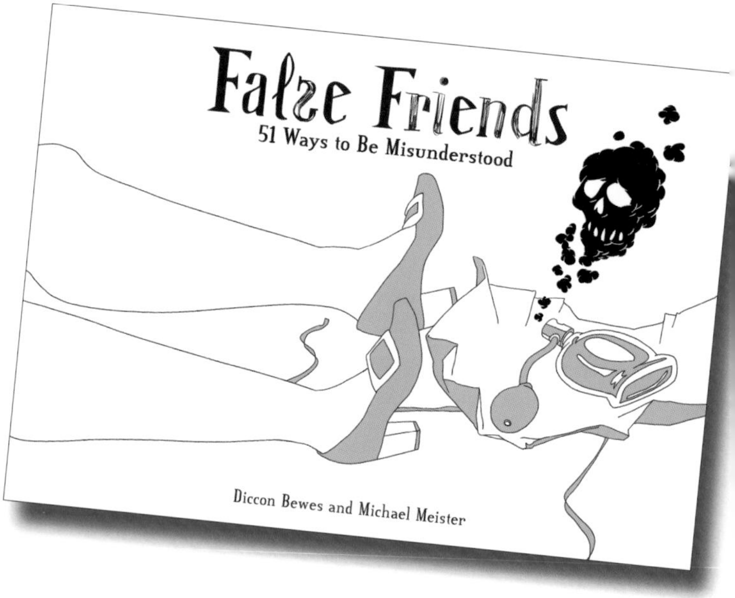
False Friends
51 Ways to Be Misunderstood
Diccon Bewes and Michael Meister

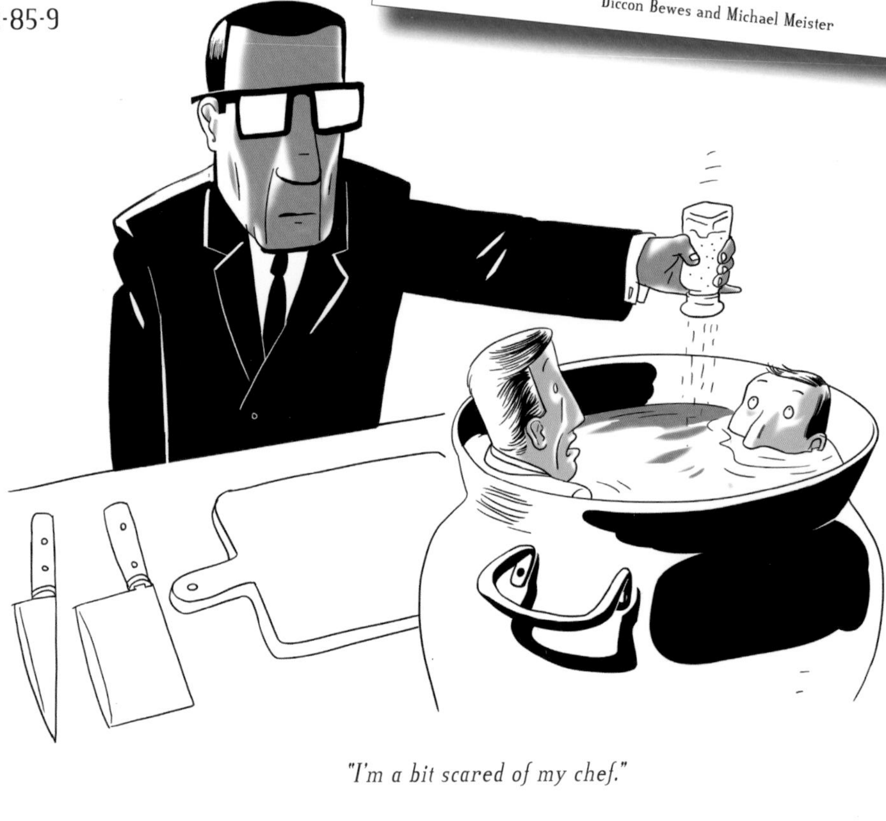

"I'm a bit scared of my chef."